Sweetwater Deception

Sylvia Nickels

Sweetwater Deception
Copyright © 2018 by Sylvia Nickels
ISBN 978-0-9799222-7-5
ISBN 0-9799222-7-5

Sweetwater Deception/ Sylvia Nickels
1. Mystery fiction. 2. Women in jeopardy – Georgia – Fiction.
3. Makeup model - Georgia – Fiction. 4. Female attorney – Fiction 5. Female lawyer - Fiction

A Different Drummer Publishing

Acknowledgments

To everyone who has encouraged me all through the years to keep pursuing my dream of publication, my heartfelt thanks. I have been so fortunate to have the steadfast support of my immediate and extended family as well as the many talented writers in my writing groups. Their critiques and suggestions have been on point. If my books have any merit, it is most likely because of that support and those suggestions. Their acceptance of me as a bona fide writer gave me that much-sought-after prize of all writers, validation as a writer.

Dedication

I dedicate this book to my immediate and extended family in Georgia, those still here and those who have sadly left us, some much too soon. Without your steadfast support and encouragement I may not have continued my quest for publication when the words would not come and the formatting defied me.

I am so proud that several family members have decided to explore their own talents for writing, both prose and poetry. To them I say, write on!

Chapter One

Dana Tucker Pennington tossed a small stone into the small pond. Ripples spread out from its fall into the still water. She watched until the brackish green pond was still again, then turned back toward the house. She stepped onto the still discernible but overgrown path through the thick stand of pine trees which blocked most of the early morning sunlight. Her brand-new sneakers made no sound, softened by layers of fallen brown needles. Only an occasional flattened weed revealed her progress toward the pond just ten minutes ago. Like the memory of her past life in Sweetwater County. Could she build a new, maybe even happier, life back on Cattail Farm, where she grew up?

When she left the gloomy shadow of the evergreens, the white, freshly painted farmhouse gleamed in front of her. Shoulders drooping, she paced slowly over the narrow grassy open space between the trees and road. Reliving memories of the breakup with Bret had drained her. Coffee. That's what she needed. Her back stiffened as she noticed a silver-gray Lexus standing in the driveway. A man came around the corner of the house. He must have gone around to the back door when she didn't answer at the front. She wasn't expecting anyone, who could it be?

She raised a hand to block the bright sunlight and the movement apparently caught his attention. He paused in the act of opening the car door. He waited by the car while she crossed the road and the white sand of the yard.

Tall, dark haired, with gray at the temples, he wore an open-necked blue and white checked shirt. His designer jeans were well worn as were the Justin leather boots. Something about the face seemed familiar. She couldn't see his eyes, he wore wraparound dark sunglasses.

She stopped a few feet away. "Can I help you?"

He reached up and pulled away the sunglasses. She looked into eyes as green as the pine trees behind her.

Bret.

The sunlight dimmed, her knees buckled, and she felt herself falling. *So stupid, fainting here in my own yard.* Strong hands grabbed her shoulders and guided her to the porch steps.

"Sit. Head down." He commanded.

In a moment her vision cleared, but she kept her head down, willing facial muscles to a neutral expression. She raised her head and spoke, though not his name, she couldn't say that yet. "You're the last person I expected to see."

A small smile creased the sides of his mouth and the well-remembered eyes widened. "Folks still drop by to say 'Hello' and welcome new neighbors in the country."

"Neighbors?"

"You didn't know?"

She shook her head. *Would she have come back if shed known?*

"Actually, I lease your hay fields. Have for ten years."

She knew the shock she felt was mirrored on her face. *Why hadn't she read through those papers the property management agent sent? Surely the name of the person who leased the fields was on them.*

"But–you moved back to Sweetwater County? Why?"

"It's a long story. Could I beg a cup of coffee? I only had one cup before I left the house."

Anger she couldn't feel twenty-two years ago rose up in her. *How dare he waltz back into her life as though he hadn't trampled her heart? Maybe it had been a mistake to come back to Cattail Farm. She hadn't expected the strength of the bittersweet memories it brought back, especially the pond. She should have raged at him then, screamed and cried. Called him names for leading her on. She might, eventually, have gotten over him.*

A curt refusal rose to her lips. Something in his eyes stopped the words. *That day at the pond, he'd told her he was sorry, but what was between them was over. His eyes had said something else. Now they held an expression that she couldn't read. Replacing the sparkling animation she had loved, patience and understanding were in their azure depths.*

She knew somehow that if their paths parted again, he would not enter her life a third time.

Curiosity mingled with her anger. Why had he moved back to Sweetwater County? Why had he leased her hay fields? Was he still married? She slammed a mental door on the rebellious spear of hope that tried to spring out.

Chapter Two

"That's about all I can offer. But it will take a minute. I was so anxious to get reacquainted with the farm, I left without making any." She led the way through the sun porch dining area to the compact kitchen.

"That's fine. I don't have any pressing chores waiting for me."

She busied herself measuring coffee into the basket, then poured water into the drip coffee maker. In spite of her attempts to control them, her hands trembled and the cups and saucers she took from the cabinet rattled a little.

"I have bread, but the toaster isn't unpacked. I could make it in the oven. Would you like some?"

Babbling. Why was she babbling?

"Oh, no. Coffee's good." He lounged against the counter, arms crossed, left hand on top. Too near. No wedding ring. Didn't necessarily mean anything. She took a breath and slipped past him, taking napkins, sugar and milk to the table on the sun porch.

When the coffee was done, she poured their cups. With a slight bow, he motioned for her to precede him and sit down. He raised his cup, eyeing her over the rim. "So. You've come home, Dana."

"Yes. This is my home." She took a sip of her own coffee to gain time. He must have as many questions about her life as she did about his. *Okay, who's going to start?*

"I heard that your husband died. But you'd lived in Carbindale a long time."

"It was never really home. Not Rockvale, Sweetwater County."

And so empty, after Tod died. Most of their friends, they hadn't really socialized a lot, had just drifted away after Tod's death. She'd retreated from life, leaving the house only when necessary. She wondered how to fill days that stretched like an empty void ahead of her.

Returning home one day about six months after Tod's funeral she pulled mail from the box beside the front door. She paused on the threshold of the modern, split foyer home they had bought when he rose to Accounts Manager at the company. They'd had a good life in it, been a more-or-less viable part of the community, raised a beautiful daughter who never gave them a moment's heartache. If there'd been no peaks of ecstacy, there had also been no deep valleys of sorrow. It was the life she had expected with Tod. The reason she had accepted his proposal and moved from Georgia to Illinois with him after Bret broke her heart.

Among the department store and cell phone ads was a fat envelope with a Georgia postmark and the return address of Sweetwater Property Management. She took the envelope and the rest of the mail inside and put it on the table in the breakfast nook. When she slit the envelope she pulled out a copy of the County Tax Invoice for the farm. The agency had sent it to her, with the recommendation that she sell.

Certainly not, she couldn't sell Grandpa and Grandma Tucker's farm. It was all she had left of them. She felt a spurt of anger at the agent for even suggesting such a thing. He was just doing his job, of course, looking out for her best financial interest.

An idea stirred. She'd lived in Carbindale more years than she'd lived in the state of her birth. That didn't mean she had to stay there. She could sell this house, instead, and move back to the farm. She put water in the kettle and set it on the stove. Taking a tea bag from the tin on the counter and a mug from its hook, she sat down to consider the pros and cons. The pros won. She sealed the decision with a cup of Darjeeling tea.

She looked up the number of a real estate firm. That night she called Gabrielle at college. As soon as Gaby heard her voice, she asked sharply. "Mom? Are you all right?"

"Oh, yes. Fine. The house just seems so much bigger with only me rattling around in it."

"You should get out more. You've become a hermit."

"I suppose."

"You could fly here for a few days, but I'm pretty busy with finals. I wouldn't be able to visit with you much."

"I know, honey. I have something else in mind."

6

"What, then? A job?" She heard a guarded note in her daughter's voice.

"I'm thinking about selling this house and moving to the farm in Sweetwater County."

"After all these years?"

"It's where my roots are."

"Didn't you tell me no one's left except the odd cousin or two?"

"I have no family, here, either." Dana pointed out.

Gaby hesitated for a beat. "Mom, this is very sudden. And you don't know anything about running a farm."

"It isn't an operating farm, anymore. Just a couple of hayfields leased to a neighbor."

"Where will you live? Isn't someone leasing the farmhouse, too?"

"No. The agent says the family who were living in it moved to the city. That's why he recommended selling it now."

"What will you do there?"

"I don't know. Renew some old friendships, maybe. Redecorate the farmhouse. Write."

"Okay, Mom. Do what pleases you, Georgia or Illinois. After law school, who knows where I'll end up practicing?"

"Everything still going well with your classes, honey?"

Gabrielle's voice quickened. "Yes, Professor Dalling told me he'd write a great recommendation for an internship this summer. His old college roommate is a partner in a prestigious firm here in Nashville. Keep your fingers crossed."

"Always, darling."

"Well." Gaby still sounded doubtful. "Just keep whatever you want of my old stuff, Mom. It'll be years before I can think of having a real place. Let me know if I can help."

Gaby had a final on motions and pleadings to study for so Dana let her go and broke the connection.

She had known that all of her furniture would not fit in the farmhouse. So she'd driven down a month before her move to arrange a good cleaning for the rooms and decide what to keep. Gabrielle's baby crib and rocker, a few other keepsakes, could be stored in the old corn crib. She had no plans for children, Gabrielle said, but she might change her mind.

She didn't tell Bret she'd almost changed her mind after her house was sold. She'd leafed through a glossy magazine at the pharmacy while standing in line. A model in a full-page cosmetics ad caught her eye.

Susan! It can't be. She's over forty, now. Is she still this beautiful? No, this girl can't be a day over twenty-one. A daughter? Bret's daughter?

She gasped and thrust the magazine back into the rack. But her house was sold, the closing set for the next day, new owners ready to take possession. So she went through with it and walked the empty rooms once more, then locked the door behind her.

With a feeling of burning bridges, on a bright September day she drove away from Carbindale for the last time. She'd booked a room at the only motel in the nearby town of Rockvale. Next morning after a fast food breakfast and coffee, she met the movers and directed their unloading. Barely three months after she decided to return to the farm, the deed was done.

She spent the rest of the day unpacking personal belongings and enough kitchen items to make a light dinner. She'd remembered to pick up bread, milk, and a few other food items at the last supermarket she passed on her way from Rockvale. A grilled cheese sandwich and bowl of canned soup was her first meal in her new/old home.

The interior of the house looked the same as it had when she was growing up. The only difference was the light and airy dining area. Her grandparents had installed window walls around ten feet of the long back porch, extending the tiny kitchen. They enjoyed showing it off when she and Tod stopped by with baby Gaby on their delayed honeymoon the year after they married.

Eleven months after their visit, her Grandfather succumbed to pancreatic cancer. Dana returned with Gaby, now a toddler, to help her Grandmother, who had slipped and fallen two weeks after her husband's funeral, breaking her hip. The break refused to heal and she passed away in her sleep just three months later. She was anxious to join Grandpa, Dana thought. Losing them both so close together was a terrible blow, but a husband and two year old baby girl left little time for grief. She engaged the property management firm and had never returned, except for the cleaning trip, until now.

Too tired to walk around outside after her meal as she'd planned, she washed her few dishes and put them away. She locked up and switched off lights, thankful for electricity and well water at least. Phone and cable hookups would take a week or so. Gabrielle could reach her on her cell phone in the meantime. Glad she'd made up the bed earlier, she dragged on pajamas, brushed her teeth, and climbed between the sheets. She fell asleep before she'd read two pages of her paperback copy of a recent bestseller.

Chapter Three

Morning sunlight woke her early and she determined to renew her acquaintance with the farm where she'd roamed fields and woods as a youngster. Breakfast could wait. She donned jeans and a long-sleeved shirt. Brand new sneakers completed her ensemble and she started out, feeling a nip of fall in the September air.

"And then, when I returned from the pond, here you were. Looking for all the world like the country boy you used to be." It wasn't true, though. The only time she'd seen this heaviness in his eyes was that day at the pond. Unable to meet that somber look, she glanced through the wraparound windows. The massive oak tree no longer stood at the edge of the yard, providing refuge from the hot Georgia sun. She had a vague memory of Grandpa telling her about the terrific storm which felled it the year he died. At least that reminder would not greet her through her bedroom window each morning.

She had loved only the lean, good-looking Bret Kenyon since she and Susan, her school friend, were in eighth grade, he a lofty senior. He graduated, his family moved away, and he disappeared from her life. Susan took accelerated and summer classes, finished high school a year ahead of Dana, and took a job in Atlanta.

A few times during Dana's senior year her friend and party-girl Susan Kent persuaded Dana to visit her in the city and go out dancing. She only went in the faint hope of running into Bret. During one of those visits her wish came true. In the crush of a crowded disco floor, she and Bret were thrown together. The magic was still powerful for her. She thought he felt it, too.

He drove out to the farm often that spring and summer. On one of his visits, after a picnic at the pond, they paused under the huge tree in the side yard. He faced her, a hand spread on the rough bark on each side of her and leaned close, green eyes sparkling with laughter. "We're now destined to be together, dainty, dazzling Dana." Her heart danced, buoyant with ecstatic dreams. Remembering, her breath caught in her throat, again.

What happened to our destiny, Bret? What would my life have been like if you'd meant those words? Why did you break my heart?

"Oh, spoons. I'll be right back."

"I don't need..." She escaped to the kitchen, knowing full well they didn't need spoons, since they both drank their coffee black.

This morning, the very idea that Bret Kenyon would be drinking coffee at her table within the hour would have–would have... But there he was, she could see the tanned profile of his strong jaw out of the corner of her eye.

The fragrance of honeysuckle filled her nostrils. She looked down at the fragrant blooms on the twig she had stuck in the pocket of her shirt. The hardy though destructive vine she loved twined over bushes and saplings. It's sweet scent drew her across the road when she had started out earlier. A gentle breeze sighed through the pine trees well into overgrowing the old pasture. A quarter mile past the site of the old barn and through a thinner copse of pine trees, had been the small body of water she'd named Cattail Pond as a girl. She had decided to call the farm she'd inherited Cattail Farm. Was the pond still there?

She'd walked slowly along the faint path through the pines, finding the pond did still exist. It seemed smaller and shallower, maybe because the patch of cattails thrust up tall brown spikes over fully half of its area now.

She reached to pick one of the sausage like tops. As she tore it apart, she saw again the silky fibers that spilled from Bret's fingers that day by the pond. They dipped and floated on the fall breeze, not dropping to the ground, as she had felt the pieces of her heart were doing.

"I'm sorry, Dana. I'm in love with Susan. We're getting married next week."

She pushed the scene out of her mind and took a deep breath. Time for some questions of her own. She grabbed the first two spoons that came to hand and returned to the porch. He gravely accepted his soup spoon. "Thanks."

"Your turn, Bret. You've been leasing my fields for ten years?"

"Since I bought the Tate property down the road. Got tired of calling it the 'old Tate property' and named it Mill Creek Farm. I run some Charolais, keep a few horses, even a couple of goats."

"Does Susan like the country?"

He hesitated. She held her breath.

"Susan disappeared. Took off when our baby girl was just a few months old."

Her heart lurched. A few months. Less than a year after he broke up with me to marry her.

"Why didn't ..." She started to ask the question she longed to have answered. Then stopped in realization.

He nodded. "By then you'd married Tod and were the mother of your own daughter."

His voice was even, but she sensed strong emotions held in check, like the storm raging in her own spirit.

Did he really love Susan? If not, why did he marry her? And had he remarried? He must have looked for me, he knows when I married, about Gabrielle. If I'd waited. No, the past can't be undone.

"If I could have found her, it would have been hard not to break her neck." He paused. "I ran ads, hired private detectives I couldn't afford, nothing. In the end, I divorced her on grounds of abandonment and was awarded sole custody of Heather."

"Your daughter. She's what—twenty-two now? Does she live here in the country with you?"

"Rarely." The hint of their remembered sparkle softened his green eyes. "Hates the country. She went to boarding school, usually found something to keep her in the city during the summer. She did some modeling while still in school, did well and loved it, and decided that was what she wanted to do."

"Where is she now?"

"New York. She was lucky enough to land with a great agency. She's getting some good assignments."

"Would I have seen her in anything?"

"Maybe. One of her ads ran in a national magazine."

The one I saw and mistook for Susan.

"Was it hard for you, to let her go to New York?"

"Yes. We keep in close touch, though. Talk often."

"That's good." They were silent for a few minutes, lost in thoughts of the past.

He stood and walked over to the open hutch. She'd placed a few pieces of her grandmother's china on it, along with an enlarged snapshot of Gaby loading her pickup for college. His gaze lingered on the picture of Gaby. "In college? Where?"

"Graduated from UGA in Athens. In her second year of law school at Vanderbilt now. I had a bout of pneumonia that kept lingering just before she began first year. I practically had to push her out the door. She wanted to try for delayed entry and stay home to take care of me."

His expression immediately showed anxiety. "Are you okay? Any recurrence?"

"It was an unusually cold and wet early fall. I'm perfectly fine."

"Good." He touched the photo. "She's very beautiful, like her mother at that age. And even now." He smiled, the first real one she'd seen this morning, and she felt the breath squeezed from her lungs.

"We're out of coffee. I'll bring the pot out here." She jumped up and fled to the kitchen again. Berating herself for feeling such juvenile confusion, she stood trying to regain her composure, palms on the counter. She sensed his presence behind her and, as though it were the most natural thing in the world, slipped into his reaching arms.

His mouth sought her lips hungrily. Their kiss wiped away the pain of the years apart.

"My darling. My dearest. I prayed you'd come back." He murmured against her cheek, kissing her eyelids, her forehead, then claiming her lips again.

"Would you have come to me, if I hadn't?" She asked, when she could speak again.

He raised his head, with a broad smile. "You probably won't believe this."

"Believe what?" She kissed the fingers that traced the curve of her cheek, then twined in her soft hair.

"I had a plane reservation to Carbindale. I was going to find out once and for all if we might have a future now. On the way to the airport, I stopped in at the Property Management office to sign the contract for next year. The agent asked me if I knew you were moving back to the farm."

"You're not serious?"

"Cross my heart. He looked kind of strange when I floated right through the door, clicking the heels of these old boots."

Awash in happiness, they returned to the porch, forgetting the coffee. They cuddled on the wide window seat and lost all track of time. At last physical hunger overpowered their drive to rediscover everything about each other.

"I really have very little to eat in the house. We could go to Rockvale." She suggested.

"I'm not ready to share you. I've food at my house. Come on."

He started to drag her out to his car.

"Wait. My purse, my phone." She grabbed her purse from the night stand in her bedroom and they left.

Chapter Four

When they entered the old Tate farmhouse, she marveled at his renovations. "It's beautiful. Who would have thought this lovely old wood was under the grime Old Man Tate let cover it? Grandma and I used to bring him stuff from her garden, her meat loaf he loved, a cake or pie."

She also discovered that Bret was a very competent cook. They devoured his eggs Benedict with mushrooms under the striped umbrella on his sunny brick terrace. Finally, hands clasped so tight that his knuckles whitened, he spoke. "There's something else, Dana. You deserve to know."

Her heart lurched. She wasn't certain she wanted to hear any more, remember more pain from the past.

"I loved you so, Dana. Not Susan. I hoped it would help you to get over me, even hate me, if I told you that."

"Why?" She cried, before she could stifle the word.

"I'd told my roommate, who it turned out knew Susan, I was going to ask you to marry me. He insisted on a final singles bash for me at a friend's place."

She resisted the urge to put her hands over her ears. The roaring in them almost drowned his next words anyway.

"I had a couple of beers, one rum collins with Susan. I can't swear it was spiked, but we both passed out. I woke up, or came to, next to her on the bed." He took a deep breath. "She woke, too, while I was dressing. I was angry, hungover, she just shrugged, asked for a lift home. No one else was around."

Dana suspected what was coming next. She stood and took their cups to the kitchen and poured the cold coffee down the sink. Refilling their cups, she went back to the table.

"A real friend to both of us, wasn't she? You don't have to..."

"I need to tell you. But if you'd prefer not to hear it, I understand."

He took the cup of hot coffee. When his fingers brushed her hand, she knew she had to hear it all. "Go ahead. So it was a setup. And Susan was part of it?"

"I can't be sure. Two months later, she came to see me. She was pregnant, she said, and what was I going to do about it? I asked the usual dumb questions—how did I know the baby was mine? She laughed. Did I remember waking up in bed with her? She wanted money for an abortion, but I wouldn't hear of it. And that's when I came out here and broke our engagement."

He leaned back in his chair, looking at the ceiling. Somehow she knew there was another shoe to drop, and it would be harder to accept than what he had just told her.

"Telling you that was the hardest thing I've ever done, and the worst day of my life. But there's something I may have to tell Heather someday that will be just as hard."

Dread was in the green eyes when he raised his head and looked at her. "She's been my daughter since I held her in the delivery room. I raised her, nursed her through colds and kissed her boo boos when she fell down. Can you guess what I might have to tell her?"

"You're not her biological father. "She guessed.

He nodded gently and sadly. "Her daddy in every way but that."

"How did you find out? Did Susan tell you who the father was before she left?"

"I doubt if Susan knew. I discovered she was pretty dependent on alcohol and pills after we married. I did some investigating, found out a couple of the guys had sex with her, too, that night, then dragged me to the bed. I just assumed that I—that..."

Dana touched his hand. "Then how..."

"In her senior year of high school, Heather was badly injured in a car accident. She needed blood. Naturally, I wanted to give her mine. But I couldn't. Tests showed our blood was totally incompatible, there was no way I could be her father." Even now his voice was ragged with the pain of finding out his daughter was not his flesh and blood.

"Bret. I'm so sorry. How did you keep it from her?"

"Swore everyone who knew to secrecy. Threatened all kinds of lawsuits if they told her."

Through an open window, she heard cattle lowing. A flock of geese took to the air from a rest in the nearby pasture. She opened her mouth to speak–she didn't know what–and the telephone rang.

"Should have forwarded my calls." He picked up the cordless phone.

It was Heather. Dana could hear her excited news. "Dad! I made the final auditions! Can you fly to Athens tomorrow morning?"

"Congratulations, baby. Final auditions at company headquarters, then?"

"Yes. You can, can't you?"

"Of course. We'll be there."

"We? If you're bringing someone, I'll arrange another pass."

"Thanks, honey."

"Dad. Keep all your fingers crossed. I want this. I'll fax the schedule times and where I'll be staying. Gotta go. Love ya, pop.

"Love you, baby. See you soon." He set the phone down and turned to Dana.

"Lady Veronica Cosmetics has been searching for a new signature model. Heather's made the final cut. Final auditions in Athens, at the home office. You'll come with me?"

"If I can find enough of my clothes. Run me home so I can start searching through boxes?"

"The two women I love most, meeting each other at last." He grabbed her hand and pulled her into his arms.

"Bret. I have to find something to wear if I'm going..." Her lips were captured again. They surrendered without a struggle.

In his office off the kitchen another phone rang once, it cut off, and an electronic beeping sounded.

"Heather's fax." Bret walked both of them through the door, still raining kisses on her face, neck, and hair. They reached the machine and he picked up the sheet of paper. He held it so she could see, too, and read aloud. "'Athens, final cut 10:00 am. Pick up passes at front desk, Lady Veronica headquarters, noon. We have suite reserved at the Southern Inn, near airport.'"

He grinned down at Dana. "Hmmmm. We could have a problem."

She smiled, shaking her head. "I'll be staying at the Hospitality House at the University. As a grad, Gaby can still use it."

He slapped his forehead. "Gabrielle. Can she cut classes, you think? I'll fax Heather for another pass."

"Maybe. I'll call and see. But you have to take me home so I can find my clothes, Bret. Now!"

"Let me send this and we're outta here." He took a fax sheet and scrawled a request to Heather for another pass, then keyed in the number on her cover sheet.

Chapter Five

At her door, he let her leave his arms with reluctance and checked his watch. She had insisted she hadn't enough time to go out to dinner. Unearthing appropriate clothing, removing any wrinkles, if she could find her steamer, and packing again would be time-consuming.

"I cook, love. I'll fix salads, grill salmon steaks, bake a couple of potatoes. We'll make it an early evening and have my company chopper pick us up at seven in the morning."

* * *

They stood near the windsock pole at the corner of his helo pad next morning, watching the yellow and green helicopter set down. Ducking under the whirling blades, they climbed into the cockpit. Raising his voice to be heard over the engine, Bret introduced the pilot, Jon Blessing, a small man in his thirties. He wore a uniform which matched the helicopter's colors and set off his darkly-tanned handsome face. Thin lips parted in a friendly smile, revealing perfect teeth, and he gave her a warm handshake.

She enjoyed the flight, but, having been away so long, could only recognize major landmarks like Stone Mountain. They were walking through the concourse at the airport when she heard a familiar voice.

"Mom, Mom. Wait." Gabrielle rushed up and threw her arms around her mother.

Dana returned her daughter's exuberant hug, then held her at arms length, not missing the faint circles under the long-lashed sapphire eyes. "Been burning the midnight oil, I see. And you must have gotten up very early."

Gabrielle laughed. "Nope, drove down last evening and stayed at H House. And I intend to know more about pleadings, torts, briefs, what-have-you, than any lawyer who ever graduated from Vanderbilt. Who did you say this is and who else are we meeting?"

"Gabrielle, Bret Kenyon, a very old friend from Sweetwater County. We're meeting his daughter, Heather, at the Lady Veronica building."

"No way! Heather Kenyon, the Georgia girl with the inside track to be the next Lady Vee sig model?"

"The same. We're keeping our fingers and toes crossed." Bret looked from Dana to Gabrielle. "You two could be sisters."

"Sure. Except Gaby is three inches taller, ten pounds lighter, and has more hair, darker, too."

"Details. Come on, let's see if Lady Vee sent a limo to pick us up."

"As a matter of fact, I saw a liveried driver holding up a sign with the name 'Kenyon' printed on it. Never dreamed I'd be riding in the thing." Gabrielle took her mother's bag and led the way to the main entrance.

The three climbed into the luxurious vehicle. The driver stowed Bret's and Dana's luggage in the back after telling them that he would leave the bags with Lady Veronica Security. Fifteen minutes later he deposited them at the Lady Veronica building, which appeared to consist entirely of glass and polished black marble, covering an entire city block.

The lobby's elegant appointments were hardly visible for the people jamming the room. Most were from the media and all seemed to be talking at once, some into microphones, others into tape recorders.

Bret cleared a way through the bedlam to the receptionist's desk, Dana and Gaby followed. After repeating his request to the harried receptionist three times, he gained possession of three passes to the further regions of the building. One of two uniformed security agents stepped away from the desk and led them to a locked elevator. Using his key, he opened the door, pushed a button, and told them someone would meet them upstairs. When the elevator door closed, the quiet seemed almost deafening.

The noise level when they emerged from the elevator did not quite match that downstairs, but it was loud. A whip thin woman, black hair piled in braids on top of her head and wearing a designer suit in Lady Veronica lavender stood waiting for them. She beckoned for them to follow her. They stepped into the huge dressing room. Wearing a velvety lavender towel and seated in front of a lighted wall mirror sat Heather Kenyon, attended by four women and one man dressed in lavender coats. What looked like hundreds of bottles, jars, spray cans, and assorted beauty implements stood on the counter, and their mirrored reflection doubled the number.

"Daddy!" Heather waved and blew kisses, requiring the woman who had just applied her lipstick to remove and redo.

"Your party will have to return to the other room now, Mr. Kenyon. Miss Kenyon is being presented to the world in half an hour as the new Lady Veronica signature model. After the press conference, at the reception, you will be able to visit with her." The thin woman led them out of the room.

"I am impressed. But no way would I go through this." Gaby gestured around the room.

"Nor I. But she seemed to be enjoying it, didn't she, Bret?" As her mother enjoyed attention. She shook the thought away.

"Oh, yes. She's used to a certain amount of this hoopla. I think this is a little over the top, though."

Surrounded by Lady Veronica executives, Heather soon emerged and walked to the dais that bristled with microphones. She looked regal and serene in a slim, lavender-beaded gown, a black diamond choker, and earrings. The company president presented her to the room full of top fashion reporters. The light level in the room increased exponentially as photographers captured the lovely image which would grace countless newspapers, magazines, and news broadcasts.

The crowd adjourned to a dining room where long tables held numerous varieties of canapes, hor d'oerves, tiny sandwiches, fruits and vegetables with dips, and a lavish bar.

A phalanx of lavender-coated employees escorted Heather to her father. She still wore the beaded gown, but Bret enveloped her in a bear hug anyway. They smiled with deep mutual affection. Bret reached for Dana's hand and pulled her beside him.

"Heather. This is Dana Pennington. And her daughter, Gabrielle."

"Thank you for coming. I'm sorry to pull Daddy away. It's my only chance to spend a little time with him. We'll meet again, I hope, and we can talk."

"I'll call you from the hotel. Dinner. Eight." Bret called as they were swept away to meet a VIP. Heather smiled and winked at Dana and Gaby.

Soon the official contingent left, taking Heather and Bret, and the crowd began to migrate to the main elevators. Dana and Gaby followed.

"I guess we're on our own for transport, now." Dana tried to flag down passing cabs, but all were full.

Gaby held up a key ring. "Don't despair. I brought my pickup over and parked a half block up the street, then took a cab to the airport. I knew there'd be mobs of press here."

"I'm impressed, and grateful, at such forethought, darling."

"I'll take you to H house and we'll freshen up. I know a great place for dinner. Bret will be buying, right, Mom?"

In the truck, Gaby glanced at her mother, grinning. "Do I get to know what's going on with my mother? You're back in Georgia one day and being flown around by this hot, good-looking guy."

"You'll hear all about it at dinner. Watch the traffic, Gaby."

Chapter Six

At eight, Bret was not waiting for them under the ivy-covered overhang of the Southern Inn as he'd confirmed when he called Dana earlier. After the doorman had given them several dirty looks, and Bret still hadn't emerged from the lobby, Gaby drove on around to a parking space.

"Maybe he fell asleep, I'll ask the desk to ring his room."

"Ms. Kenyon called and left a message for you, Mrs. Pennington." The desk clerk pulled an envelope from a pigeonhole and tried to hand it to Dana. She stared at it, unable to take it. Not again. Her heart clenched so hard in her chest, she gasped for breath. Gabrielle reached past her mother and took it from the clerk's hand.

"Thanks." She took her mother's arm and guided her to a sofa. "Mom? What's wrong?"

"I can't look at it. Open it, please, Gaby."

With a puzzled glance from her mother's white and drawn face to the envelope, Gaby slid a finger under the flap and ripped it open.

"There's been an accident, Mom. Heather says we should get to the hospital right away."

"Wh-what? What kind of accident?"

Gaby crammed the letter into her backpack and took her mother's arm. She half-dragged her to the hotel entrance and out to the truck. They were headed toward the hospital by a shortcut Gaby knew before she said any more.

"We'll find out more when we get there. Just hang on, Mom."

"Gaby. Is it Bret? IS it?" Dana twisted in her seat belt, staring at her daughter. "Tell me."

"An eighteen-wheeler slammed into the limo as they entered the freeway. The impact was just where Heather and Bret were seated. She's just bruised a little, Bret is—injured."

"Oh, my God. Hurry, Gaby, hurry."

Weaving in and out of traffic, driving as fast as she dared, Gaby smiled briefly. "We'll be there in a few minutes, Mom."

True to her word, seven minutes later, Gaby drove into the ER parking area. They were out of the truck the instant she slammed the gear shift into park and cut the engine. As they rushed through the automatic door, they spotted an island of lavender and headed that way.

The thin, black-haired PR woman who had taken them to the dressing room to see Heather only a few hours ago was in the group. Dana pushed through to her and touched her arm. "Heather Kenyon's father, how is he?"

The woman turned, shock in her eyes. "Who are—Oh, you were with her father. It's bad." She gestured toward double doors leading out of the ER. Heather Kenyon paced near the doors, her lavender beaded gown flashing in the lights. As Dana and Gaby hurried toward her, a doctor in green scrubs spotted with blood, pushed through one of the doors. Heather grabbed the woman's arm. "My father. How is he? I want to see him."

"He's lost a lot of blood, Ms. Kenyon. We have a limited supply of his type. You can help most by going to the lab and getting typed. Unless there's some reason you wouldn't be able to donate?"

"No. I'll do anything to help. Where's the lab?"

Dana stopped short. Oh, God. She can't find out this way, too.

Gaby bumped into her. "Are you ok, Mom?"

"We'll go, too. In case he can use ours." Dana touched the girl. Her slender arm was so tense it vibrated like a live electric wire.

Dark eyes filled with fear looked into hers. "Thank you. Please help me hold together. I can't lose my father."

In the lab, a skillful technician required only moments to draw a vial of blood from each of them. "If you want to wait, we'll know if the patient can use any of your blood in a few moments."

Five minutes later, she returned and motioned for Gaby to come to the counter. She consulted Gaby's papers. "You're Miss Pennington. Type A Negative. Correct?"

Gaby nodded.

"It's fortunate you're here. Come with me, please."

Heather looked puzzled. "I'm A Positive. How could that be if Dad is A Negative? But if Gaby's is better for him, thank God, she's here."

Half an hour later, the three returned to the emergency room. They waited and watched the Lady Veronica contingent field questions from the media. A few reporters called out questions to Heather, but she only shook her head. At last, the same doctor came through the doors again, the strain that had been on her face now gone.

"Ms. Kenyon. It looks as though your father is going to be okay. We've stopped the bleeding. The two units of his blood type we had on hand, along with that from the donor, were enough to replace the blood he lost. You can see him for a few minutes, before we take him to ICU, at least for overnight."

"We'll wait in the cafeteria, Heather. Go."

Gaby had gone for a refill of their coffee when Dana saw Heather crossing the dining room toward their table, Lady Veronica personnel trailing her. She dropped into the chair beside Dana and put her hands over her face. Dana touched the girl's shoulder and squeezed. Her face looked so drawn and stricken. "He's going to be okay. I'm sure he probably looked worse than he is, with the IV's and all."

Gaby, having seen Heather arrive, returned with three coffees, just in time to hear her reply.

"She said he can't be my father." Tears squeezed from under her tightly closed eyelids.

"The doctor? What exactly did she say?"

Heather raised her head as her stunned, wet eyes went from Dana to Gaby. "He is my father. He was in the delivery room when I was born. He raised me, after my mother left. He's always been there for me."

Dana felt she could have strangled the doctor as well as the long-departed Susan with her bare hands. She hesitated. Did Heather suspect that Bret knew? How much should she tell her, until Bret could fill in the rest?

"Excuse me." Gaby spoke briskly. "I'm still in the dark about most of this, my Mom and your Dad."

"Gaby. I'm sorry." Dana apologized.

"It's ok. But, I think you better tell us both what you know, Mom."

Chapter Seven

Dana took a deep breath. She reached for a hand of each girl. "Bret and I were in love and your mother and I were friends, Heather. But, Susan became pregnant through a situation I won't go into right now. Bret married her, thinking he was responsible. After the accident when you were in high school he found out the truth. But he loved you dearly, you are his daughter, and he made the decision to keep it from you."

"Yes. He is my father. I don't care what blood tests say." Heather choked.

"And you can still be his own true daughter, Heather." Gaby said.

"What do you mean?"

"He can adopt you."

"But I'm an adult."

"Doesn't matter. Easier, in fact."

"Easier? How?"

"Don't have to try and find biological parents."

Heather's face shone. "Adopt me... The same as he would have if he'd found out when I was little." A shadow crossed her face again. "And they'd still been together."

"Sure. It's done all the time."

Dana laughed and reached for her daughter's hand. "You're going to be a great lawyer, Gaby."

"Of course. With a famous sister, I think. But right now d'you suppose you can get free makeup for a struggling law student, Heather?"

* * *

Bret's hospitalization dragged out longer than expected when he developed a stubborn staph infection. Super antibiotics eventually banished it enough that he was released a month after the accident. After his release he had no lack of loving care and Dana also finished exterminating the infection with her favorite homeopathic remedies.

"They should have let you be a consultant on my case. I'm a lucky guy, a beautiful fiance' and a great doc, too."

Dana put a finger on his lips. "Shhh. The medical profession doesn't appreciate folks who prefer natural treatment to drugs."

Both hale and hearty by the Friday before Saturday's Halloween, they thoroughly enjoyed dressing up as Queen Guinevere and Knight Lancelot for his company's party. And reprising the roles for the neighborhood children as they rang the doorbell for trick or treat the next night.

Early in December Dana and Gaby decorated the house at Cattail Farm with abandon, then helped Bret with his farmhouse. Heather was able to make a flying afternoon visit and add her touch.

Thanksgiving and Christmas were magical holidays for the Penningtons and Kenyons. It was a whirlwind season for Heather. Lady Veronica kept her to a heavy shooting schedule as their signature model. She begged her father and Dana not to marry until she could be home long enough to have a real part in the occasion. Bret loved her enough to acquiesce even though he was so anxious to take Dana as his wife at long last.

Between decorating and Christmas shopping, Dana and Gaby anticipated the most gala season they could remember. They sandwiched in preparations for what was intended to be a small April wedding at Cattail Farm as they prayed for good enough weather. But somehow the wedding showed signs of becoming the social event of the spring season in Sweetwater County.

After attending a beautiful Christmas Eve church service Bret, Dana and Gaby sat before a crackling, wood fire and sipped eggnog. The full long-needled pine from Bret's property sparkled with lights and ornaments above mounds of gaily wrapped gifts.

Gaby laughingly handed Bret a small box covered in red and green striped paper. "We always open one gift on Christmas Eve."

"Well, I guess that includes me if I'm going to be part of this family." He replied, pulling off the matching bow.

Dana watched and felt a tear threaten, blinked it back. If only he knew. But she couldn't say anything. Maybe never.

She swallowed the lump in her throat. "Hey, where's mine?

Heather managed a couple of hours with them next day and then the Lady Veronica helicopter whisked her away again.

They spent a quiet New Year's Eve. Heather was in New York City as a guest on numerous TV specials. She called just before midnight, before she had to leave for yet another party, said she missed them terribly. She then flew cross country for an appearance at the Rose Parade.

A short bout with pneumonia felled Dana the last of January. This time since Gaby was between semesters and was free to be with her during the illness. Heather called to commiserate but said she couldn't get away. On Valentine's Day Bret showered the women he loved with candy and flowers. Dana received her favorite yellow roses, chocolate truffles and dinner at the Top 'o the Tower Restaurant in Atlanta.

By the middle of March most of the wedding preparations were done. Old friends threw a couple of parties for the bridal couple, who insisted that only their friends's presence and good wishes were needed.

As the big day, the sixteenth of April, approached, they crossed fingers and hoped Heather could be with them for several days.

She did get to Atlanta and called when she arrived. "Dad, I'll be out to the country as much as I can, but they're keeping me pretty busy."

"Baby, we're proud of you. But we are so hoping you can spend some time with us."

"I know and I will. For sure the rehearsal dinner and wedding. Can't miss that! Gotta go, Dad. Bye."

The day of the wedding dawned bright and sunny, a perfect early spring Saturday in Georgia. The area all around the pond had been cleared, the cattails standing tall and green. When Dana walked between the rows of seated guests toward her groom she thought her heart would burst with happiness. All painful memories of that long-ago day at the side of this same pond were swept away.

Later during the reception at Bret's farmhouse she noticed Heather on the patio talking on her cell phone. She thought her stepdaughter seemed agitated, one hand clenching the delicate yellow fabric of her bridesmaid gown. But when the photographer wanted one more group picture Heather seemed her usual gorgeous, animated self.

Finally Jon whisked the newly married couple to Hartsfield International Airport to board their flight to Arizona for their Grand Canyon and points west honeymoon.

Chapter Eight

Mom! How was your flight?" Next day Gaby listened for a moment as her mother's happy voice traveled through the ether from Grand Canyon. Late afternoon sunlight poured through the farmhouse window panes, painting a golden path across the living room's polished wood floors.

"I know. The Big Ditch is something else. Wait'll you see it from the bottom."

Another pause. "Oh, yeah. I have great news. Professor Dalling's pal came through. They're taking me on as an intern this summer until I start third year in the fall. And they may let me work part-time while I finish law school, too!"

"Well, I should think they'd recognize the value of a lawyer who's at the top of her class." Dana Pennington Kenyon always expressed appropriate pride in Gaby's achievements. "You have to finish your second year. Then the internship, and I'm happy for you, but who knows when we'll see you again!"

Hearing the dismay in her mother's voice, Gaby said, "I know. But they'll be adding a couple other new interns and they want to start us all at once." She added. "I won't be here when you get back from your honeymoon. But I'll try and get back for July Fourth."

After relaying Bret Kenyon's congratulations Dana told her that they were about to go to the hotel dining room. Her new husband was starving, airlines didn't serve food the way they used to do.

"Okay. Feed my stepdad. Talk to you both soon. Bye."

Gaby laid down the phone and picked up Book Three of her set of Blackstone's Commentaries. The old boy had a way with words. Many words. But before she could open the book the front doorbell pealed through the farmhouse. Then someone banged on the front door.

"Geez. Gimme time." She peered through the peephole and saw her blonde now-officially-stepsister, Heather Kenyon, on the porch. Heather raised her left hand and jabbed the bell button again before Gaby got the door open.

"Heather. Come in."

Heather rushed through the door almost before Gaby could move back. She reached up and swept a lock of hair behind her ear and turned to face Gaby. "I'm so glad you're home, Gaby. When I got here I realized you might not be."

"Did you drive from Athens? I thought I heard a car's engine while I was on the phone."

"Yes, I couldn't locate Jon or I would have had him bring me in the chopper."

"Oh. Can I get you some coffee? Tea? Mom's no wine connoisseur, but I think she has a bottle of Zinfandel maybe."

"Yes. No. I don't want anything."

"What's wrong?"

"Maybe nothing. I don't know what to do. Where is she?"

Confused, Gaby asked. "Where is who? Mom? She and your dad are on their honeymoon, of course, at the Grand Canyon."

Heather shook her head, the lock of hair escaped and she pushed it behind her ear again. She paced to the sofa near the fireplace, threw her Gucci bag down on Gaby's law books, whirled and crossed the room again. "Susan didn't show up."

Watching her step-sister Gaby had a momentary flash of the one time she'd seen Heather on a fashion runway and then her words sank in. "Susan? Your mother? Didn't show up where?"

"The hotel. She said she had something important to tell me. And she's not answering her phone."

"You talked to your mother? Recently?" This was the first Gaby knew Heather wanted to meet with her runaway mother.

"I tracked her down. I-I didn't want Dad to know. I couldn't hurt him."

As Gaby stared at her, the doorbell shattered the silence in the house again.

This time three men stood on the porch. One was a nice-looking man wearing a dark suit and another the uniform of a Georgia State Trooper. The trooper had a firm hold on the upper arm of the third, a man in handcuffs.

The one in the suit asked, "Gaby Pennington?"

"Yes. What...."

The one who had spoken glanced at Heather. "And you're Heather Kenyon?"

"Yes." A look of alarm crossed her face as she looked at the handcuffed man. "Has something happened to my Dad?"

The suited man ignored her question. "When did you last see your brother here?"

"Brother? This man is my Dad's pilot, Jon Blessing. I haven't seen him for two weeks. I asked you about my Dad."

The handcuffed man spoke, sorrow in his voice, "Heather. I'm sorry. I just wanted to be able to see you occasionally. She was going to tell you the truth."

"The truth? What are you saying, Jon?"

"Ms. Kenyon, I'm sorry to tell you. Your mother's body was found outside a hotel in Atlanta. This man was identified as having been with her shortly before the attack. He tells us he is your brother."

"Susan dead? Jon? What's he talking about? My brother?'

"Ms. Kenyon. We'd like for you to come with us to the city, please. You can get all the details there." The man hesitated, seeming unsure whether to continue. Finally did. "I'm sorry for your loss."

Heather said. "Thank you. But until two days ago I hadn't seen my mother since I was about six months old."

Gaby spoke up. "Excuse me. Why do you need to talk to my stepsister? Is she a suspect."

"You may come, too, if you like, Ms. Pennington."

"Neither of us is going anywhere until we see some identification," Gaby said, voice firm. She gave a pointed look at the uniformed State Trooper's badge, making note of his name. She moved her gaze to the man in the suit and waited.

He sighed and pulled his identification folder from his inside jacket pocket, flipping it open. The name on it was Detective Sergeant Jud McAlester with the Atlanta Police Department and the picture matched.

"All right. Detective Sergeant McAlester. Would you please come in and tell us what this is all about?" Gaby stepped back.

She indicated the sectional sofa, which was somewhat out of place in the farmhouse. Between her rekindled romance and courtship, and illness and then the wedding her mom hadn't had time to replace it. The state trooper and Jon Blessing sat on one end, Sergeant McAlester on the other.

"A woman was murdered, Ms. Pennington. We believe this man might have been involved. He was apprehended here in Sweetwater County a few miles from here." He looked from Gaby to Heather. "He tells us he is your brother, Ms. Kenyon. Is he?. If not, who is he and what do you know about him?"

Gaby and Heather exchanged puzzled looks. Gaby nodded for Heather to answer.

"As I said, Sergeant. Jon is my father's pilot. If he's claiming to be my brother, I don't know why. And I want to know why you think he might have –hurt–my mother?" She ended on a questioning note.

"I would prefer to do this back at the station," McAlester replied.

"I'm sure." Gaby muttered, sotto voce.

McAlester gave her a sharp glance. "This is a murder investigation, Ms. Pennington. You're a law student. I'd expect you to be more cooperative."

Gaby crossed her arms and stared back at him. She hoped her expression didn't reveal her surprise that he seemed to know as much as he did about her family. When had Heather's mother died? "Perhaps I will be when I know a little more than the bare fact that Heather's biological mother has been killed. And that you suspect her father's pilot of being involved. She has told you she had not seen him in two weeks and is puzzled as to why he claims to be her brother."

McAlester shifted a little in his seat. "I can get a warrant that compels you both to return to Atlanta with me for questioning."

"Yes, you can. Until you do that and unless you intend to arrest us on the spot, I suggest you take your prisoner and leave my home."

Heather waved her hands. "Wait, please. When did my mother die?"

McAlester hesitated. "Her body was discovered in an alley behind the Buckhead Emerald Tower about four a.m. today."

"If she was—deceased—how did you determine that she was Heather's mother?"

"That's all I can say at this point, Ms. Pennington." He looked at Heather. "I ask you again, Ms. Kenyon. Will you voluntarily meet me at the Atlanta police station to continue this conversation? Of course, you may bring an attorney, if you wish. Though you must know that Ms. Pennington cannot function as your official attorney."

Heather looked at Gaby. "But I want her to be with me. If she thinks an attorney is necessary, I'll call my father's law firm to send someone."

"Very well. I'll expect you to meet me there within two hours." He nodded to the state trooper, who rose and pulled Jon Blessing to his feet. Jon cast a beseeching look toward Heather as he was led to the door.

Chapter Nine

Gaby pulled into the Atlanta Police Station visitor parking lot and turned off the car's ignition. She hadn't tried to keep up with Detective Jud McAlester's vehicle. She had expected the state trooper to peel off at the intersection to reach State Police headquarters near Rockvale. Instead he continued to bring up the rear of their short procession, apparently transporting Jon to lock-up in Atlanta. She looked over at Heather and reached to pat her hand. "Rotten way to find out about your Mom's death. Not that there's a good way."

"That's not all." Heather pulled a strand of blonde hair and twisted it around her finger. "I'm so confused. What in the world did Jon mean, telling them he's my brother?"

"Hopefully we'll find out something soon. Shall we go in?" Gaby threw her backpack over her shoulder and opened the car door.

Heather sighed and got out also. They walked toward the imposing brick building. The fairly new police headquarters was ten stories high, only the lower five floors had large windows and they looked a little odd. Gaby supposed they might be bullet-proof. The next two floors had a few smaller windows. The upper three floors had even few windows and they were recessed, covered with an iron mesh.

Is Jon Blessing on one of those floors? Surely not. McAlester didn't say he was charged with Susan's murder, only a suspect. Why? Surely they had some reason to suspect him. Sons, if he was Susan's son, don't routinely kill their mothers. At least I sure hope not.

The two young women entered the wide lobby and walked toward a long counter below a huge sign with the word 'Information' printed in large letters. A woman in uniform stood behind the counter and listened to a man who was obviously under the influence of either drugs or alcohol who leaned on the desk talking in a loud voice. "I know my rights. I need to see my daughter."

"Sir, you are not on her visitor list. I suggest you leave now or that officer over there will arrest you and you also will find yourself in a cell."

"You'll hear from my lawyer, can't keep me from 'm daughter," the man turned and almost collided with Gaby. "Women," he slurred, "give 'em lil' power." He glared at Gaby as though she'd run into him.

She shrugged and ignored him. Turning to the officer behind the counter, she said, "I'm Gaby Pennington and this is Heather Kenyon. Detective Sergeant Jud McAlester asked us to come in to talk about one of his cases."

The woman nodded. "He just came in, I'll let him know you're here."

Gaby and Heather moved back to let an older couple speak to the officer. The woman's eyes were red-rimmed and she held a shredded tissue in one hand, her other clutched the handles of a large tapestry bag. The man spoke. "Our son–," his voice broke and he began again. "We were told that our son was brought in for questioning a few hours ago. We want to see him, please."

"What is his name, sir?" The officer's hand hovered over her computer keys.

Gaby and Heather walked toward a row of plastic chairs near a side wall. Just as they reached it the officer on the desk called, "Ms. Kenyon, Ms. Pennington, Sergeant McAlester will come down for you in a couple of minutes."

Gaby turned back and replied. "Thank you." They took two vacant seats in the second row of chairs.

Heather sat for a couple of minutes, then jumped to her feet. "I can't sit. Why hasn't Dad returned my call?"

"They're probably in a spot with no cell service. He'll call as soon as he can. Maybe it's best he doesn't until we know more."

"God! I hate to do this to them. They're on their honeymoon."

"You didn't do it, Heather. Whoever–hurt your mother did it. You don't think..."

"Of course not. I've known Jon since I was twelve. He couldn't murder anyone. I'm sure." But her voice wavered just a little on the last two words.

"What about–if he's..."

Gaby was interrupted as Sergeant McAlester approached them. "Ms. Kenyon, if you'll both follow me we'll go to my office."

They followed him to a painted steel door with a security card slot beside it at the end of the long counter. A buzzer sounded as he swiped his ID and he pushed open the door. They entered a corridor and turned right, almost immediately stopping at an elevator alcove. McAlester punched the call button and held the door for them. He touched the 3rd floor button and when the door opened again they stepped into a corridor with numerous doors, some closed and some open. McAlester led them through one of the doors into a huge room which held dozens of desks and an equal number of cubicles separated by gray half walls.

McAlester stopped at a cubicle halfway across the room and indicated they should enter. "Have a seat. Can I get you coffee or a soda? Water?"

"No, thanks." They both answered as they sank into the two chairs in front of the desk."

"I just want to know what's going on," Heather burst out.

"I understand." McAlester replied. He moved a tablet closer. "For the record, please, your name is Heather Kenyon, your father is Bret Kenyon, prominent businessman of Atlanta, and your mother is–was–Susan Kenyon." He looked at Gaby. "And you are Gaby Pennington, second year law student at Vanderbilt? Your mother recently married Mr. Kenyon, correct?"

"They are on their honeymoon as we speak,: Gaby replied. "You seem to have looked up our families."

McAlester nodded. "Now Ms. Kenyon, again, I'm sorry for your loss. But you say you saw your mother two days ago. Will you tell me how that came about since you also said you hadn't seen her since you were a baby."

"She called me a couple of days before Dad and Dana were married. I was shocked. We hadn't heard anything from her since she left. Dad tried to find her, but couldn't. I–I wondered if she was still around. If–if she ever thought about me. But I never mentioned that to Dad."

"Why not?'

Heather seemed to sense something in McAlester's question. "Why?" She snapped "I wasn't about to have him think he had been less than a wonderful father. She abandoned me when I was not even a year old. My father has always taken wonderful care of me."

"Jon Blessing claims he is your brother. What do you know about that?" McAlester reminded her.

"I don't know anything about it." Heather crossed her arms. "Susan didn't say anything about having a son."

"You know, don't you, that Bret Kenyon is not your biological father?"

Heather's head snapped up. "How do you know that?"

"We have your hospital records from your accident in high school and Mr. Kenyon's records from his accident late last year."

Her eyes narrowed. "And Jon Blessing's?"

"Not yet. He has voluntarily given a blood sample. We will know soon if he is probably telling the truth about being your sibling."

Gaby interjected a question. "Does Jon Blessing claim that Susan is his mother?"

McAlester glanced toward Heather. She asked, "Well, does he?"

"Yes. Now, back to my original question. Tell me about your meeting with your birth mother."

"I was at home for a few days between shoots to take part in the wedding. My phone rang and a woman said, 'Heather?' I asked 'Who is this?' She said 'I'm your mother.' I almost hung up. But before my finger pressed the button, I changed my mind. I asked what her name was, and she said, 'Susan.' Then I kind of lost it. I screamed at her, asked why she was calling me now, it was way too late to be playing the mother card. She said, 'I know, I know. I just want to be sure you're all right. He said you... I saw that your father and Dana are finally getting married. I'm glad. I hope they'll be happy.'" Heather's voice broke off, she looked into space.

"And?" McAlester prompted.

Heather looked at him, came back to the present. "She said, 'He said' and broke it off and said that about Dad and Dana. Did she mean Jon?"

"What do you think?" McAlester tapped on his tablet.

"How would I know? First my mother calls out of the blue and then a man I've known as a friend since I was a child is claiming to be my brother. What in God's name am I to tell my father when he calls?"

"I know this is difficult, Ms. Kenyon. But we have to find the truth about your mother's death. You eventually agreed to meet her, I take it?"

"Yes. She asked me to meet her in the Emerald Tower's lobby coffee shop. It was–strange."

"How so?"

"Like looking in a mirror. And seeing what I would look like in twenty or so years. She's–was–still beautiful. We both just kept looking at each other. But I don't think she really felt much for me, regret, happiness to see me. I don't think she was the motherly type."

"Did you sense any hostility? Anger?"

Heather hesitated. "No. Nothing like that."

"But something?"

"It doesn't sound so good. But what I got a sense of was–sort of–calculation. Like she was sizing me up for some reason."

"Do you now believe that you sensed accurately?"

"Yes. In the business I'm in, I run into it often."

"Any idea what that reason might have been?"

Heather shrugged. "No. But she was a stranger to me. It was hard to tell what she was really thinking."

"You've done quite well as the signature model, I believe they call you, for Lady Veronica Cosmetics. And your adopted father is a quite successful businessman. Do you think she might have been 'sizing you up' toward asking for money?"

Heather's expression of dismay answered McAlester's question.

"So you did wonder about that. Did you ask her?"

"No. After it occurred to me, I just wanted to leave. So I did. I got up and walked out of the coffee shop."

"While you were with her, did you ask her who she meant, who she referred to, when she started to say 'he said?'"

"No. I was only with her five minutes, tops." Heather clasped her hands tightly together in her lap, stared at the detective. She swallowed and said, "You haven't said how my—how Susan died."

McAlester looked down at the file on his desk. "We won't know for sure until after the autopsy. Evidence points to blunt force trauma to the head."

"With what?" Gaby asked.

"I can't say." He replied, then suddenly shot a question to Gaby. "Had you ever met Susan Kenyon, Ms. Pennington?"

In spite of herself Gaby felt her eyes widen in surprise. "No. I was born in Illinois and I was a new baby and later toddler the only times I was ever in Georgia. Before now, I mean." She hesitated. "She may have been still here then, but even had Mom and Dad seen her I certainly wouldn't remember it."

Jud McAlester tapped another note into his tablet. He glanced at Heather. "You're a little older than Ms. Pennington, right?"

"Yes, not quite a year. What does that have to do with anything?"

"We have to ask a lot of questions. Some of which end up having no bearing on the investigation." He replied in a soothing voice. "No offense to either of you."

Gaby touched Heather's hand. "Sergeant, we'd like to go home now. If you have any further questions for us please call or come to my Mom's or Heather's father's farm." They stood up and McAlester did also.

He said, "I'll walk you out. This place can seem like a labyrinth."

Chapter Ten

They reached Gaby's truck and as she started the engine Heather's phone rang. Heather looked at the caller ID and breathed. "Thank God."

She depressed the answer key. "Dad, you got my message." After she listened a few seconds, she said, "We're okay. We've just left the detective who's investigating–her death. Where are you and Dana?"

She looked at Gaby, and mouthed, "Checking out."

Then into the phone, "When do you arrive?" She listened again.

"Ok, we'll pick you up at the airport." Paused. "No, Dad, Jon can't pick you up."

She looked helplessly at Gaby. "He's–Jon's being held by the police. It's kind of a long story."

"Dad. Why don't you and Dana get checked out and to the airport. Call back when you're there if you have time, or call when you're airborne. We're both fine. I'll tell you what we know when we talk again. Love you. Be safe. Bye."

"So, home or stay in town?" Gaby asked.

"Their connecting flight is due to land at three a.m. Lady Veronica keeps an apartment in town for visitors. I'll call Keira and see if anyone is using it."

Heather touched a speed dial button and spoke to the head of publicity at Lady Veronica headquarters. She ended the call after a moment, a puzzled look on her face. "She said it wouldn't be possible for me to use the apartment but didn't give a reason. And then said she had another call and just cut me off."

"Has she done that before?"

"Never. Gaby? What's going on?"

"I'm sure it's nothing. Corporate types get bent out of shape easily." Gaby tapped the steering wheel for a second. "I've a friend who has a small place out near the airport. He's visiting his family up north for a few weeks. We can crash there." With that decided she drove toward the entrance to the parking garage.

They stopped at a deli to pick up salads for a meal neither felt she wanted. "I only had a piece of toast for breakfast and it's almost seven now. I bet you haven't eaten either?" Gaby looked at Heather, who shook her head. "Better add two tuna salad croissants to the order." Gaby told the clerk, pulling out her wallet.

A few minutes later they arrived at a small, slightly rundown complex about a mile from the airport. Gaby pulled into the space in front of a studio apartment sporting a windchime made of several lengths of metal pipe painted in iridescent swirls beside the entrance. Gaby retrieved a key taped to the wall behind the wind chime and opened the door which wore wide stripes in primary colors.

When Heather made no mention of the retro décor, outside or in, Gaby realized her step-sister was too tired to notice. Faint shadows under her dark blue eyes emphasized her pallor.

"Come on, let's wash up and try to eat something. We'll be better able to deal with all this." Gaby pointed to the bathroom door and walked over to deposit their food on the tiny kitchen table.

After a few minutes Heather came out of the bathroom and sat in one of the two rickety chairs. "Good thing I'm not scheduled for a photo shoot for a few days. I look half-dead." As she heard her own words she looked stricken. She put her hands over her face.

Gaby hugged her and ignored the words. Thinking it would help if Heather had something to do, she said, "There's usually a few soft drinks in the fridge. Be a dear and pour us a couple of glasses, okay?"

As Gaby took her turn in the bathroom, Heather rose and opened the compact refrigerator next to the sink.

They picked at their salads and tried to think of something to talk about besides the thing that was uppermost in their minds. Finally Heather could contain herself no longer. She burst out, "Why now?"

Gaby raised an eyebrow in question.

"Why did she call now? Why wait until I'm nearly twenty-four? What kind of woman was my biological mother?"

"We'll probably learn some of those answers in time." Gaby studied her step-sister's face, looked deep into her eyes. "Sis, you might not like some of the answers. Maybe you should try and prepare yourself for what might come out."

Heather's fork stabbed into the styrofoam salad container as she dropped it. "What did you say?"

"I said maybe you should try and..."

"No." Heather's eyes filled with tears. "You called me 'Sis'. Gaby, you can't know how much that means to me."

Gaby smiled and winked. "Well, before I knew where sisters came from, I begged Mom to find me one."

Heather swiped her eyes and gave a watery smile back. "I tried to match Dad up with any woman who had a little girl so I could have a sister. Now I'm glad he didn't go for it."

"I guess some wishes do come true, though, huh?" Gaby pushed her chair back. "Now I suggest we grab a few hours sleep before we pick our parents up."

Heather picked up their food containers and placed them back in the plastic bag they'd brought in. "Sleep. I doubt it. You take the bedroom and I'll see if there's an old movie on the idiot box. If I get drowsy I'll pull that throw over me on the sofa."

"I'm pretty strung out, too. I can stay up with you."

"No, I'm ok. Go ahead and get some rest. Sis." Heather grinned and gave her a shoulder hug and a little push.

Chapter Eleven

Gaby gently touched Heather's arm a few hours later. Heather's eyes flew open. She looked around and after a few seconds seemed to remember where she was. "I guess I dozed after all. Is it time to go to the airport?"

"Yes, I thought we'd get there a little early in case their flight was early."

"Yeah. Sometime if they catch a tail wind, they do get in early." Heather rose in one graceful movement and began to fold the throw and place it on the back of the sofa.

Gaby replaced the key behind the wind chime after locking the door. She stowed their trash In back of the seat and backed her truck out of the parking space.

"Dad said he'd arranged for a car to take us back to the farm." Heather said as she buckled in. "Will you leave the truck in long-term parking?"

"No. I'll follow. A bunch of my law school stuff is piled in the back there. I might need it."

"Oh. Okay, I'll ride with you."

"Glutton for punishment, aren't you?" Gaby grinned.

"The truck's ride is fine. I just thought it would give the newlyweds some privacy. They haven't had much of that since the wedding."

"True, that. And nice of you to think of it." She hesitated. "Not many women in your situation would be so generous." She threw a mischievous glance at her passenger. "Being a diva, and all."

Heather reached a hand up to flip her hair and gave a mini-preen. "Well, I try to be a nice diva, you know!"

But she immediately deflated again, her mind obviously returning somewhere else.

"He was pretty shocked, I guess." Gaby decided they might as well talk about the elephant in the truck with them.

Heather said, "To say the least. He could hardly believe what Jon said. He wants to go see him tomorrow. In jail, if they're still holding him. Do you think they will be?"

Gaby shrugged. "Unknown. We still don't know why they think he's involved in Susan's–death."

"Her murder." Heather whispered. "My birth mother was murdered."

They were silent while Gaby negotiated the metro roadways to reach the airport. Just as she pulled into the entrance to the short-term parking lot, Heather spoke again. "Why would someone murder her? What's in her past that would lead to such a horrible thing?"

Gaby wasn't sure she expected an answer so she waited until she'd driven up one lane and down another, finding an empty space about midway along the second lane. "The police will find out, I'm sure. It could have been a random act. Unfortunately Atlanta has its share of those."

"I suppose." They stepped out of the truck and Gaby clicked the fob. "But then why would they think Jon had something to do with it? How did they even connect him to her?"

"Maybe your dad will find out something tomorrow. I don't know him well yet but I'd bet he's trying to find out something right now."

"Oh, yes."

They reached the main entrance to Hartsville International and headed for the Mid-South Airways counter. According to the arrivals board behind the harried ticket clerks, their parents's plane would land in five minutes, right on time. They stepped on the people moving beltway which would take them to the passenger arrival area.

They found seats and sat for a few minutes to wait. Heather was quiet, seeming lost in thought. She turned to Gaby. "I want to go to her home. Maybe there's something to help explain what happened."

"I would think that's doubtful, Heather. The police will have gone over it."

"Even so. If she hid something that would lead to her killer, I might find it and they might not."

Gaby examined her stepsister's beautiful face. "Why do you think so?"

"Whether she wanted me or not, I'm her daughter. We probably have–had–similar thought processes."

"I suppose that's possible." Gaby said. "Do you know the address?"

"She gave it to me. I almost threw the slip of paper away. I can't imagine why she even gave it to me."

A thoughtful look came into Gaby's eyes. "I wonder." She rose from her seat. "Let's get closer so we see them as soon as they come through the gate."

As both scanned the milling crowd, they spotted a man in a chauffeur's uniform holding up a sign with the name "Kenyon" printed on it. Pressing their way to him, Heather explained they were waiting for the Kenyons, too, that Mr. Kenyon was her father.

The tall, clean-shaven man didn't try to keep the admiring look from his dark eyes as he looked at the two young women. "Mr. Kenyon ordered the car from the plane. Did he know you were meeting them?"

"Oh, not to give them a ride. They'll take the car. We're going to follow."

He looked relieved. "Okay."

Gaby stood on tiptoe, then raised her arm, waving. "There they are. They see us."

In a few minutes the four were hugging and talking over each other. The driver took the handles of the two wheeled carry-ons Bret had dropped and said, "Folks, if you'll follow me. I need to get the limo out of the reserved area so others can get in."

"Of course. Lead on," Bret checked the driver's name on the small brass rectangle pinned to his jacket, "Laurence."

"You girls are riding with us, aren't you?" Bret asked his daughter, a worried crease marked his forehead as he examined her face.

"No, Dad. Gaby has her truck, we'll follow and see you at–which farm?

"Ours. I want to see if Jon left any kind of message in the last few days. There was no phone message when I checked it remotely."

Both vehicles pulled into the driveway at Cattail Farm, the farm Dana Pennington, now Kenyon, had inherited from her grandparents. When she reclaimed it she also reconnected with the man now her husband. Gaby parked beside the sleek black limo. She and Heather got out of the truck and walked to the car. Their parents left the limo and met them.

"Sure you won't change your minds? There's plenty of room at our house, you know, girls."

"We know, Dad. But you and Dana should have some time alone. You've had precious little since the ceremony."

"It's sweet of you both. But I think we'd be just as happy with all of us under one roof." Dana said.

Heather turned to Bret. "Dad, you said you were going to try and see Jon in the morning. I want to go, too."

"Oh, honey. Maybe you should wait."

"I'd like to go, too," said Gaby.

Everyone turned toward her in surprise.

"Well, I am going to be a lawyer. I could, might, be of some help."

"She's right, Dad." Heather agreed.

"If everyone's going, so am I," Dana declared.

"Okay, you all seem determined. I'm outnumbered. Shall I have the car service send a car and driver out? Or I could drive us in the SUV or Lexus."

"Maybe we should use the car service. You've just flown across the country, twice," Heather said.

"All right. Then we'll talk in the morning. Or I should say, later this morning." They all hugged good night and both younger women climbed the steps to the front door. Bret and Dana got back in the limo. He must have told the driver to wait until they were inside. Through a front window Gaby saw the car's taillights flash when it pulled back into the road after she and Heather were behind the closed door.

Chapter Twelve

At ten o'clock Gaby and Heather walked wearily into Bret Kenyon's beautifully restored farmhouse. Dana Pennington Kenyon sat at the table in the small dining room off the kitchen. Her hands were clasped around the cup of coffee in front of her.

"Mom, you must be so tired." Gaby massaged her mother's shoulders gently.

Dana touched her daughter's hand, and replied, "I'm sure we all are tired, honey. Did you two get any sleep?"

"We napped 'till time to go to the airport. And a little more at the house. Did you manage any on the plane?"

"A little. And we attempted to rest here, too. Not too successfully, I'm afraid. Bret's trying Jon's home phone again."

"Sit. I wanted to ask you, Gaby. Are you still going to DC–" She broke off as her new husband entered the room. "Anything, Bret?"

"No. McAlester asked us to come to headquarters, to his office, and he'd see if I could see Jon. He's not sure if Jon has actually been charged with anything. Thinks he may still just being held for questioning as a 'person of interest.'"

He walked over and looked into his daughter's face, adding, "There was a call from him on the log here but he didn't leave a message." After hugging Heather and Gaby, Bret ran his hands through the dark hair just showing a few strands of gray.

"So bizarre." Heather shook her head.

Bret held her again for a moment. "It is. We'll find out what's going on."

He looked at the clock. "The driver for the car service should be here any minute. I arranged to have him and the car all day. Maybe we'll know something after we've talked to the detective. And, hopefully, Jon."

"Is Jon being held in the same building?" Heather asked.

Bret glanced through the window and said, 'Here's our ride. Everyone ready?"

They were all silent for most of the forty minute ride into Atlanta, each lost in his own thoughts. All four were still weary from the long night and the aftermath of shock at the news of Susan's death.

At one point, Heather looked at Gaby beside her on the rear facing seat. "Your Mom said something about you going to Nashville. Do you have to go?"

Before Gaby could answer, Dana spoke, "Yes, honey. I wish she could stay, but she starts an internship with an important law firm Monday, so she needs to go."

The driver, a different one than the one who drove them from the airport, dropped them at the front of the police station and Bret handed him some bills. "Get something to eat, or whatever, and I'll call you when we're ready to go."

"Not necessary, sir." The driver indicated the cash.

"Yes, but take it." Bret waved it away.

The four walked into the station and spoke to the same information officer Gaby and Heather had talked to the day before.

She also told them the same thing, to wait for a few minutes, Detective McAlester would be down to escort them upstairs. Twenty minutes later Gaby spotted the detective making his way toward the section of chairs where they sat. "Here he is."

McAlester led the way, not to his office, but to a small room with several molded chairs. A woman in uniform sat in the chair nearest the door.

"Mrs. Kenyon, Ms. Pennington, if you will wait here for a little while. I want to speak with Mr. Kenyon and his daughter in another room."

The four exchanged looks, Gaby was the only one who didn't seem surprised at the group's separation. Bret touched Dana's arm, said, "I'm sure we won't be long, honey."

After they left with McAlester, Dana gave an almost accusing look at her daughter. "You expected that, didn't you?"

"Well, yes." She sat beside her mother. "It's standard protocol. Speak to people one at a time."

"So they can see if stories vary?" Dana's voice had a dry tone. "Since I did once know Susan, I'm surprised they let you stay with me."

Gaby shrugged. "Anything I told them would be second-hand, so I guess they figure it doesn't matter."

"Poor Heather. It must be so hard on her."

Gaby nodded. "She seems happy to have more family to stand with her though. Of course, Bret will always be most important."

They lapsed into silence, conscious of the listening officer, who leafed through a magazine.

Chapter Thirteen

Jud McAlester had stopped at another office and asked Heather to wait there with a Detective Collins, his partner. Bret objected, wanted to know why. His daughter was understandably upset by her mother's murder and should stay with him.

"We won't be long. If Ms. Kenyon needs you, Detective Collins will let us know."

Bret reluctantly went with McAlester to his office. McAlester's phone buzzed and he asked Bret to sit, he'd be right back. Bret narrowed his eyes when McAlester returned and sat behind his desk. Bret wasn't used to being told to sit and wait for anyone. He suspected that McAlester knew that. Maybe he even suspected that Bret was somehow implicated in Susan's death. Though he knew, of course, since Bret and his new wife had been miles away and forty thousand feet in the air he couldn't have been physically involved. Bret realized McAlester was talking and two words had penetrated his thoughts. "Excuse me? What did you say?"

"I asked if you were aware that your ex-wife was a high-end call girl, a prostitute?"

"What?"

"So you're implying you didn't know?"

"I'm saying I didn't know. I assume you know this for a fact or you wouldn't say it?"

"Yes. Tell me what you do know about your ex-wife. How long you knew her, where you met, etc."

"I'd be very surprised if you didn't already know, but okay. I knew Susan since high school. She and—she was two years behind me. But she took accelerated classes and graduated just a year after I did. She left Rockville to come to Atlanta and look for a job, so she told—Dana. I was taking summer classes to get a head start on my second year of college."

Bret didn't like thinking about that summer. He twisted in his chair. "Is this relevant to my ex-wife's murder?"

"We have to gather a lot of information in every case and then sift through it."

"I appreciate that, Detective. But it was over twenty years ago that we were together here in Atlanta. How can that have anything to do with it?"

"We're not sure. And can't be until we know her, and by extension, your full story."

Bret sighed. "A college friend, more of an acquaintance, brought Susan to a party. She...," he stopped suddenly as a piece of a puzzle he hadn't thought about in years fell into place.

"What, Mr. Kenyon?"

"She seemed surprised, almost like she wanted to turn around and leave, when she saw me. And certainly not that thrilled. Which surprised me. When we were in high school she tried to come between Dana and me. But then she started dancing and flirting with all the guys." Bret's voice trailed off again.

"What happened then?"

"Everyone got drunk, even me. Well, I thought I had. As it turned out somebody had slipped something into my drink. Next morning I woke up in bed with Susan. We were alone."

* * *

They returned to Bret's farmhouse by midafternoon, not much the wiser than when they'd left that morning.

While Bret was getting coffee from the kitchen the phone rang. Dana answered and when she hung up she wore a puzzled expression.

"Who was it, darling?" Bret came into the living room carrying two cups of coffee. He set one down on the table next to Dana's chair and touched her hair.

"That detective, Jud McAlester. He wants to come out and talk."

"We just left him an hour ago. Talk to me? Heather?" Bret asked.

"No. Well, all of us. He made a point of asking if I would be here, too."

"Oh? That's odd." Bret settled in the other chair. "Of course, you did know Susan. But it was a long time ago."

They were silent for a few minutes, both seeming lost in thoughts of the past. "Surely her death is connected to more recent events," Bret said.

"I would think so," Dana said. She paused, then continued, "The detective, he asked another odd question."

"What else?"

"He asked how long it'd been since Tod's death. What caused it."

"Really? That is strange. I suppose Tod could have run into Susan in Atlanta. Did he?"

"Yes. Actually Susan introduced us. Once when I was visiting her."

Anger darkened Bret's eyes. "Did she? After I—broke up with you?"

"No. A little while before. We bumped into him somewhere."

Bret took a deep breath, changed the subject. "When will he be here? The detective."

"In a couple of hours. About five o'clock, he said."

"Should we call the girls? You said he wanted to talk to all of us, including them?"

"He said he'd stop by Cattail Farm and speak to them."

"I'd like to be with Heather when he talks to her." Bret rose and paced to the window, which looked up the road toward Dana's farmhouse.

Dana came to stand beside him. "I know. I'd like us to be there, too. But would he let us stay in the room? They're both adults. And he separated you and Heather this morning."

"How could he prevent us from being present?" Bret asked, irritation in his voice.

She put her arm through his and leaned against him. "He could threaten to take them in for questioning. Do you think he might do that?"

"I doubt it. Then we'd have to get attorneys involved." He put his arm around Dana. "I'm sorry I snapped at you. Forgive me?"

"Of course. I knew it wasn't toward me."

"Not the beginning to our marriage we expected, is it, sweetheart?"

She sighed. "Hardly. Who would have imagined Susan could cause such disruption even after she's dead?"

Bret squeezed her shoulder. Even more puzzling, what could Tod's death possibly have to with any of it?

Chapter Fourteen

"Mom, is he there yet?" Gaby's voice betrayed more anxiety than she usually allowed.

"Sergeant McAlester?" Dana asked.

"Yes. He just left here and said he was headed to Bret's house to talk to you."

"Not here yet." She walked to look out the window. "Oh, there's his car. No time to ask you what he wanted to talk to you about. You and Heather come on down for dinner in half an hour or so. There's the bell. Bye, honey."

Dana caught her reflection in the mirror over the fireplace as she walked toward the foyer to let the detective in. She knew she would look tired, but the dark half-circles under her eyes surprised her. Something else to blame on Susan. And wished she could regret the thought sincerely. Think about it later.

"Come in, Sergeant." She opened the door and gestured for him to come in. "I'll get Bret. He's in his office."

He held up a hand. "Would you hold up on calling him for a moment, Mrs. Kenyon? I'd like to speak to you alone for just a little bit."

"All right. But if he realizes you're here, he'll probably come in here."

"I'm sure. Your husband is very protective of his family." He made it a statement, not a question.

"Of course. Why wouldn't he be?" She asked, a little too sharply, she supposed. "Have a seat, Sergeant McAlester."

He waited until she took her chair and then sat down on the love seat. "I've just left your step-daughter and daughter, as you know. Now I'd like to get a few more details from you. About your husband's business."

Dana knew her face must show her astonishment. "Tod's business? Why in the world are you asking about that?"

"I can't speak about that detail at this moment, I'm afraid. But bear with me. I understand from your daughter that he traveled a lot. Perhaps you can tell me a little more about that."

"Well, yes, he did. He was an executive with his company and was often sent out-of-state on company business."

"And how long would he usually be gone?"

"It varied. Sometimes a day or two. Sometimes as long as a week. But I fail to see what my late husband's travels have to do with Susan Kenyon, was that still her name? Her death."

"Did your Mr. Pennington know Susan, before she became Susan Kenyon?"

Dana hesitated. "I–yes, he did.. She and I were high school friends though she graduated a year ahead of me. I visited her in Atlanta. Actually she introduced us when we ran into him at a restaurant."

"At the time you were close to Mr. Kenyon, right?"

"Yes. He was home on a visit and we–got together. I'd–I'd been in love with him for years, though he considered me too young, I think. " She paused. "You might as well know, if Bret hasn't told you. He and I were very close, expecting–ah, planning to be married." McAlester apparently saw no significance to her hesitation, word change. She hoped he hadn't.

"But that summer things changed?"

She raised her head. "He came out to see me at the farm. Told me he was going to marry Susan." She hesitated again, choked the words out. "That they were in love."

"Did you believe him?"

"No. But Susan had tried all through high school to get Bret's attention."

"Even though she knew you cared for him?"

"That was Susan. She wanted every boy in school to adore her. Bret had never fallen under her spell, so I was–shocked."

"So how did you come to marry Mr. Pennington?"

"He knew Susan and Bret married. So I was available. He called me, we went out several times. His transfer to Carbindale came through. He proposed, asked me to go with him."

Dana dreaded the next question. She glanced toward the hallway, hoping Bret would stay away a little longer. She wasn't ready to tell him. Why, oh why hadn't she already told him?

"Does Mr. Kenyon know?"

Neither of them had heard his quiet tread as Bret came into the room. "Do I know what, Sergeant?"

"I was asking your wife a few questions about your late ex-wife. Have you told her how the ex-Mrs. Kenyon made a living?"

Dana hoped Bret hadn't noticed the quick breath of relief she took. She dared not glance toward McAlester.

Bret crossed the room quickly and sat beside her, arm around her shoulders. "I did. We're both still shocked. As I told you, I didn't even know she'd lived in Las Vegas. I hired detectives, filed missing person reports. She was not to be found."

"We're still looking into her history. Indications are that she had been in the business most of her adult life. The autopsy indicated more than one abortion and a tubal ligation some time ago."

"And yet, she was still beautiful, according to Heather." Dana murmured.

"Her lifestyle had taken a toll, though. She'd also had several cosmetic surgeries over time."

Bret looked at McAlester and changed the subject. "I was only able to speak with Jon Blessing a few moments today. Do you think I can see him again tomorrow?"

McAlester checked something on his phone. "Mr. Blessing will be released in the morning at ten a.m. You can make arrangements to pick him up, if you like."

"I do want to. Thank you."

"All right then. I'll go now, but we will be talking again I expect." The detective rose as the front door opened and

Heather and Gaby passed through the foyer to the living room.

They stopped as they saw McAlester. "Sergeant McAlester," Gaby said. His glance seemed to linger on her for just a second too long before moving to Heather.

Heather nodded. He was obviously not in her best graces. He stepped past the two young women as he headed for the door. "Good day again, Ms. Kenyon, Ms. Pennington."

"He always acts as though he knows something, but he'll only tell it when he's good and ready." Heather said, frustration in her tone.

"Probably a requirement for the job," said Gaby. "Let's forget him for a while. Well, after we share what he asked each of us. Something they would much rather we didn't do, it seems."

Chapter Fifteen

The three women stood at the window of the Kenyon house and watched as Bret piloted the SUV along the driveway to the turnaround in front. Bret and his passenger, Jon Blessing, emerged and walked to the front door. When the two entered the living room, Heather hesitated for a second, then went to Jon, taking his hand for a few seconds. She turned toward Gaby, "You remember Gaby, and her mother, from the wedding."

"And from last year, Heather. When you were named the Lady Veronica signature model." He nodded, "Mrs. Kenyon, Ms. Pennington."

"May I get you a drink, Jon? Coffee, soft drink?"

"A drink of good water would be great, Mrs. Kenyon. Jail water is not the best."

"No doubt. I'll get it, Dana. Make yourself comfortable, Jon. And we'll fill the ladies in on things."

"That would be a nice change," Heather muttered.

Bret returned with several glasses of water on a tray. Jon took a glass and immediately drained almost half of its contents. No one else took one so Bret set the tray on a table.

He patted Heather's arm as he passed her on his way to sit beside Dana on the sofa.

Heather leaned toward Jon and burst out, "So, are you really my brother? Or at least–half-brother? What do you know about my–our–if you are–mother?"

"Not a whole lot more than I'm sure that detective has told you. Hasn't he?"

"He told us some stuff, all right. He said she was a prostitute. Is that true?"

Jon's face twisted. "I'm afraid so, a call girl to well-heeled clients. At least for a number of years. But that vocation has a shelf life."

"But you're several years older than me. So she'd already had one child when she became pregnant with me and convinced Dad he was the father?"

Bret looked at Dana. "Do you remember when she went away for several months?"

"Of course." Dana replied. "The summer after her freshman year in high school. She told everyone she had to go help a cousin care for an elderly aunt up north. In Virginia, I think."

"I was born in Virginia. I was in foster care for almost a year when a wonderful couple, the Blessings, adopted and raised me. Their name fit them. I was lucky."

"I'm glad they did. Adopt you." Heather said, hesitantly. "So how did you find—Susan?"

"My adoptive parents were killed in a train crash when I had just turned eighteen. Their insurance and the railroad settlement gave me the means to follow my dream, become a pilot. I wanted to be free to look for my birth parents, so I took jobs as a free lance pilot, rather than try for the airlines, though the pay would have been better." He took another long drink of water.

"You looked for your birth parents yourself?" Heather asked.

"When I had time. And I hired a couple of private investigators. First one got nowhere. The second one was able to get a look at my original birth certificate and found that Susan used a fake name but her aunt's real address."

"Our great aunt, then. Is she still living?"

Bret said, "Jon was fortunate. It can take years sometimes to find any information on something like this."

"Yes, I was. And yes, Heather, she's very old and in a nursing home, but still has her faculties. Through her the PI was able to find out Susan's real name and where she was from. But Susan moved around so much, he only tracked her here, or to Atlanta, three months ago."

"So you talked to her? What was her attitude toward you?" Heather seemed to try for only curiosity, but her hands were clinched.

"Shock, mostly. She laughed. Said 'if you're glad to be alive, you have your grandparents to thank. I wanted an abortion.'" He didn't speak for a moment. "It was so callous, I was shocked in turn. It's—not a pleasant feeling to know for a fact the woman who bore you never wanted you at all."

Heather replied softly, "I know."

"I had fantasies, when I was a kid. Even though I felt disloyal to the Blessings when I did. Maybe there was a very good reason she couldn't keep me. Her family forced her to give me up, I knew she was very young. Under sixteen, her aunt said." Jon looked off into space.

Heather got up and went to sit beside her father and took his hand. "We were both lucky to wind up with loving parents, or in my case, a loving dad."

"You're right. But there's something else I haven't told you yet. I'm a twin."

"A twin?" Heather and Gaby spoke at the same time.

"Yes. My sister was adopted before I was. The couple only wanted a baby girl. Normally agencies are reluctant to separate twins, but for whatever reason , they did in our case. My private detective is still searching for my sister."

"I'm so sorry, Jon."

His lips parted in a crooked smile. "When Bret hired me as his pilot, and I met you, I nearly had a heart attack."

"Why?" Heather looked puzzled.

"You looked so much like the picture the detective unearthed of my mother. You were just a little younger than Susan was when we were born. But for a few seconds I thought I'd found my long-lost twin sister."

"If it helps, you did find a half-sister you didn't know about." Heather smiled back.

"Believe me, it does help. Knowing I'm not alone in the world."

Everyone was quiet for a moment. For all but Bret, who'd heard it on the drive from Atlanta, it was a lot of information to take in at once.

Gaby said. "I hope you all don't mind if I chime in. I feel as though I'm sort of part of the family."

"Not 'sort of', Gaby!" Heather said forcefully.

"Of course, you are part of the family," Bret said simultaneously.

"OK, thanks. I do feel it. And I know we'll be talking more about the birth and adoption and the search for Susan. But I'm curious as to why they cut you loose, Jon?" She added quickly. "I'm glad, of course."

"My alibi returned to Georgia. I'd flown a couple of young guys to Savannah the day Susan was killed. The police couldn't get hold of them at the hotel where I'd left them. So they thought I was lying. Even though I'd filed a flight plan, the whole nine yards."

Bret interjected. "I met them. Nice guys. They were so sorry for Jon's trouble because they couldn't be found. They had changed hotels because some of their buddies were there. I called in some favors and they were located."

"Thanks to your dad they were found, he had them flown back and the attorney general had to let me go."

The doorbell pealed suddenly, startling everyone. Bret went to see who was there and returned with the unexpected visitor.

Heather jumped to her feet. "Sergeant McAlester." Her tone was icy and even in jeans and t-shirt she exuded the regal disdain of a top tier model. "Back so soon?"

"I'm sorry to barge in on you. I..." McAlester began.

"And well you might be sorry." Heather crossed her arms and didn't budge.

Dana rose and indicated an empty chair. "Sergeant. We're all understandably unhappy that Bret's pilot was held by the police when he had a perfectly good alibi."

"Yes. It is understandable, Mrs. Kenyon." McAlester crossed the room and sat in the chair she indicated. "I don't want to intrude. But I still have a murderer to find. Since all of you have or had connections to the victim, you're still sources of information for us."

"How about the people she was more recently involved with, why don't you harass them?" Heather wasn't giving up her grievance against the police department.

"We are looking at them very hard, believe me." He hesitated. "There's a longstanding known police fact, the motive for the commission of a majority of assaults and murders can be traced to family or close personal contacts."

"Until they aren't," Gaby observed dryly.

Jud McAlester nodded. "This is true. If you all will bear with me, I think you might still contribute information that would help us solve this case."

"What do you mean, Sergeant McAlester?" When Heather sat back down, Bret took her hand. His other hand held Dana's hand in a tight grip.

"I believe you are all aware now of the profession that the victim, Susan Kenyon, it was still her legal name, was engaged in. She used a couple of other names, one in particular for most of her years in that life, we have discovered."

His listeners exchanged glances. Gaby spoke again. "What name did she use?"

"Susie Penny." McAlester looked at each in turn. "Any of you have any thoughts as to why she chose that as a professional name?"

Again glances and puzzled looks passed among the group. McAlester's gaze settled on Dana. Her free hand clenched the arm of her chair and her face had gone so pale Bret put an arm around her, pulling her close. "Honey, what's wrong?"

Dana jumped to her feet, spots of red on her cheeks replaced their pallor. "Sergeant McAlester, please leave this instant. You have harassed my family enough. I won't have it. I'm going to file a report with your superiors."

The others looked at Dana in astonishment. McAlester nodded. "That is your right, Mrs. Kenyon. But I am certain you want me to find the killer of Susan Kenyon. If you prefer, perhaps we could talk in your husband's office?"

"Not without me." Bret stood up. "Excuse us, Heather, Gaby, Jon." He started toward the hallway. "Coming, Sergeant?"

Chapter Sixteen

The stupefied gazes of the three younger people followed the Kenyons and the detective sergeant as they left the room.

Jon was the first to speak as they heard the office door close. "Either of you have any idea what that was about?"

Both young women shook their heads, puzzlement on their faces. A vertical frown line bisected Gaby's smooth forehead. "No-o."

Jon pounced. "You don't sound too sure. Did something ring a bell?"

"Not really." She shook her head again. "Just a vague sense of familiarity, that I've heard that name. But I can't bring it up."

"Why is he doing this to us?" Heather pounded a fist into the other palm.

"It's his job, honey. Solving a crime is messy." Jon replied.

"Well." Gaby checked her watch. "Jon! I bet you're hungry as well as thirsty." She looked at Heather. "Not trying to usurp your position, Sis, it's your home."

"No problem. Thanks for thinking for both of us. Come on, you two, let's go to the kitchen and see what we can find."

But Jon remained seated as he looked from one to the other, a sad expression on his face.

"What is it, Jon?" For the second time since he'd come in with her father, Heather walked over and touched his arm, her eyes full of caring.

"I guess I'm a little envious." He placed his hand over hers. "Gaby called you, 'Sis.' It triggered the thought again, hope of finding my – well, our other sister."

"Of course. But I know with Dad's help, we'll find her."

Chapter Seventeen

"What did you remember when I mentioned Susan's professional name, Mrs. Kenyon?"

Bret had pulled his chair around to the front of his desk. He offered it to Dana but she took one of the two visitor chairs. Jud McAlester sat in the other.

Uncharacteristic anger still simmered in her blue eyes. "It can't have anything to do with–with her murder. And so long ago."

"Please tell me. We'll try and determine if it does have any bearing." McAlester waited without saying more.

Dana sighed. She reached for Bret's hand. She looked beseechingly into his eyes. Then turned back to McAlester. "I guess there's no way to stop it? It will all come out, won't it?"

"Most likely. I'm sorry. Murder does that to survivors's lives."

Bret squeezed her hand. "Honey, what are you talking about? I'm getting the impression that I'm involved in whatever this is. Am I?"

"Yes, Bret. And I'm so sorry you have to find out this way. I've wanted to tell you. But it meant–I had to consider Gaby. What it might do to her."

A spark of comprehension appeared deep in Bret's eyes. "Maybe you could go ahead and tell me now. Whatever it is, I won't stop loving you, my darling."

By sheer force of will she kept looking at him, seeming to forget Jud McAlester was in the room. "That spring and summer. I'd loved you all my life it seemed. And that year–you said you loved me."

"With all my heart. I think I had since we sat together on the bus to school that one year. You were a shy little middle schooler. But I was the arrogant high school jock."

"You were never arrogant." They shared a smile, looking back through the years.

"You remember–the day we picnicked at the pond. And after–you shredded the cattail pod. We watched the fibers float on the breeze and you said some day we'd fly away to all these wonderful places."

"Yes. I meant it. I wanted to give you the world."

"I was giddy with joy. But between your job and classes you only had time for short visits for the next six weeks. And then I realized–I hated to tell you, I knew it would disrupt all your plans. But knew I had to the next time you came to the farm again. And that's when you told me...." Her voice trailed off.

He whispered, "Dana." Swallowed. "Are you saying... Is Gaby my daughter?"

She nodded, dashing away threatened tears. "I was devastated. But I turned it to fury to survive. Convinced myself you were the lowest of life forms. Sleeping with Susan and me, I imagined you told her you loved her and wanted to give her the world, too."

Bret's face was a study in self-loathing, his fists clinched. "And Pennington was ready to step right in. I'm sorry, I never liked him. He seemed, forgive me, but he seemed kind of sleazy."

Jud McAlester spoke softly, he knew they had almost forgotten he was in the room. "Maybe because he was. Sleazy. Or worse."

Dana turned on him, eyes wide. "What? Why do you say that? He married me to give my child a name, provided for us."

"How well did you really know him? You've told me he was gone quite a lot after you moved to Illinois. What did you know of his business affairs?"

"He was an executive at his company, they sent him out of town a lot."

"So they did. But what did he do for the company? What was his job?"

Dana opened her mouth, closed it. Opened it again. "He said his work had to do with a lot of proprietary information that he couldn't talk about. What are you insinuating about Tod?"

"He must have told you something about the company. What was their business about? What product or service did they produce? Lease? Sell?"

Dana thought she detected a faint emphasis on the word 'service' in his question. "He did call the company a 'service-oriented' business. I–I guess I was never real clear about what service it provided."

"He probably made sure of that." McAlester said.

"So, do you know? What was it?"

By the expression on his face, which he visibly struggled to suppress, McAlester did not relish enlightening her about her husband's business. He tapped a finger on his knee, finally spoke. "Your husband's business was 'service-oriented.' They provided very personal services." He paused. "Mostly to men."

"Very personal services," she repeated, "such as? And you're using the past tense. Is Constant Services not still in business?"

"No. The FBI raided their main offices in Carbindale two weeks ago, their assets seized, the owners and top executives arrested. Though most bonded out almost immediately."

Dana's face was a study in shock. All color had left it again. Bret grabbed her hand, "Are you okay, honey? Do you want some water, brandy?"

"No." She whispered. "Give me a minute. I can't believe I knew so little about the man I lived with for over twenty years."

She pulled her hand away, rose and walked to the window. She stared unseeing out at the landscaped grounds, the corner of the helicopter landing pad. After nearly five minutes, she returned to her chair, studied the carpet.

"As far as Gaby knows Tod was her father. He–it can't have anything to do with Susan. Surely. I got the idea he was just, oh, solidifying her security in her father."

"What did he do, Mrs. Kenyon? It had something to do with your daughter?"

A sudden anger filled Dana's face. "She was about three or four. He called her his 'little Susie Penny'. She would laugh and say that wasn't her name. Then he'd say, 'But to me you're my Susie Penny.' How could he?" Her face crumpled. "How could he?"

Bret gathered her into his arms, rocking and comforting her. In a few minutes she pulled back, took the handkerchief he offered and wiped her eyes.

"I thought she might have some questions, at least wonder a little, when it was her blood that saved your life after the accident in the Lady Veronica limo." She finally looked at Bret. "How will we tell her? How will she take it? And these revelations about Tod I'm almost afraid to ask more about?"

"We'll tell her together. And Heather." Bret glared at McAlester. "Don't even think about dropping this information on them first."

"Are you ready to hear more, Mrs. Kenyon? I am sorry to have to shatter your memories."

Dana sat up straighter, squared her shoulders. "I'll deal with it. Somehow. With Bret's help. Tell me the rest."

"After giving birth to her twin son and daughter, Susan returned to Rockvale, finished school. Did she seem to have more spending money, have more expensive clothing, or a car, at any time after she returned?"

"Now that I think about it, yes. The following summer, she wore much nicer clothes than before. She said she was working part-time, taking care of the wife of an attorney at the county seat. I believed her, even though she was only fifteen. She'd always taken care of her younger brother while her mother worked, until her mother remarried. She even bought a car during her junior year."

"And she moved to Atlanta immediately after leaving high school. Did you keep in touch?"

"A little. Phone calls. She made occasional visits back to Rockvale. By the time I was a senior Bret and I were dating and I visited her once in the city, mainly because I hoped I might see him." Her eyes held a soft look as they caught her husband's gaze, remembering. "Susan introduced me to Tod. He asked me out, made some reference to Susan's work–but he backed off when I said I was taken."

She turned back to McAlester. "Why did you asked about her having more money after–she went away and had her baby? Babies."

"According to an informant Susan Kent Kenyon began working in the sex trade early. As she blossomed she apparently made contact with people who ran exclusive call girl rings and similar facets of the business. One of those contacts appears to be the man you married, Tod Pennington."

Dana gasped and her hand flew to her mouth. "No. It can't be. Your informant is wrong."

"I'm afraid not. It's true. He ran the operation in Atlanta. That's how he met and recruited Susan. She'd caught his attention when he made a visit to Sweetwater County. She was still in high school, free lancing the local country club set." He glanced toward Bret, back to Dana. "When you visited Susan in Atlanta, was it her idea?"

"I wanted to go, hoping to see Bret, as I said. But she invited me often. Why?"

"You said Pennington asked you out. What did you not say when you broke off that statement? You started to say 'he made some reference to–something.'"

Dana looked down at her lap. A little pinkness stained her cheeks. "He asked if I liked Susan's apartment. Said if I moved to Atlanta he could help me get a nice place, too."

"And you didn't want to say that because you now realize–what?"

"Maybe... maybe he was going to try and recruit me, too." She whispered.

"That's probably a good guess," McAlester's voice was soft. "That is not a reflection on your character, Mrs. Kenyon. Traffickers and their more twisted clients like to get their hands on lovely, wholesome young girls."

Chapter Eighteen

Dana and Bret watched as Sergeant McAlester got into his car and drove away. The detective had left the house via the outside door to Bret's office. They turned away from the window and left Bret's office also. They stopped short in astonishment as they reached the kitchen doorway.

Heather had wrapped an apron twice around her tiny waist and presided over a couple of saucepans on the cooktop as steam rose around their lids. Gaby peeked at what appeared to be a large roast in the clear glass convection oven. Jon distributed plates and silverware around the dining room table.

Bret shook his head, smiling. "Honey, I do believe we have three budding chefs in our kitchen."

"And they seem to be rather competent, don't you think?"

"I do. I vote we keep them. Something smells very good."

Heather waved a wooden spoon toward the powder room that opened off the back door mudroom. "Wash up, you two. Dinner's almost ready. Five minutes."

"One of the chefs seems a little bossy. Maybe we should do as she says." Bret pulled Dana toward the mudroom.

A few minutes later they were seated at the oval dining table before five place settings of fine china, snowy napkins and glowing silver. Bret reached for Heather's hand on his left and Dana's on his right. Gaby and Jon completed the circle as Bret offered a fervent prayer of thanks for the food and the family circle. He did not fail to ask for the blessing that Jon should find his twin sister very soon. After 'Amens' sounded around the table, Jon looked at Bret. "Thank you. From your mouth to God's ear."

After the food was passed around and each had assuaged their appetite a little, Gaby spoke to her mother and

Bret. "Can you tell us what Sergeant McAlester wanted to talk to you about in private?"

Dana laid down her fork, sighed. "I know you're anxious to know. Could we wait until after dinner and gather in the living room for coffee before we talk about it?"

"Sure, Mom." Gaby glanced around, gathering agreement from Heather and Jon. She added, "We found a frozen chocolate cheesecake in the freezer. And there's whipped cream."

"Perhaps it should have stayed in the freezer," Dana said.

Heather pointed to Jon, disappointment plain on his face. "We can diet another day."

When they were seated in the living room, dishes cleared and in the dishwasher, coffee cups in hand, Gaby cast an expectant look at her mother.

"How do I start?" Dana looked deeply into her daughter's eyes. "Before I do, I ask you to forgive me, darling. I hope you can."

"Mom. Forgive you? You've been a wonderful mother, I couldn't have asked for a better."

"I hope so, baby. Let me ask you, do you remember the anniversary of your–father's and my marriage?"

"Well, yeah. Why?"

"And your own birthday, of course. Did you ever–count the months between?"

Gaby gave an uncertain grin. "Well, yes. When I was a teenager. I realized that either I was born early, which you never mentioned, or well, you were pregnant when you and Dad married."

"I knew you must have, even though you never said anything about it. I was pregnant, yes.

"As far as I remember the subject of your–father's blood type never came up in family conversation either." She paused, as a faint look of dawning comprehension appeared on her daughter's face.

Dana was so focused on Gaby, she didn't notice the same look on Heather's face. Heather reached blindly for her coffee cup and her fingers tipped it over. Coffee flooded the side table and dripped onto the floor. "I'll get–get a towel." Heather jumped to her feet and ran from the room. Jon sat without moving, looking a question from one to the other of those remaining in the room.

"Dad–wasn't my Dad, was he?" Gaby finally got the words out.

"I am so sorry, I should have found the courage to tell you long before now. I just.... No. But he knew I was pregnant. And that Bret was the father. He said he wanted to marry me anyway, give the child his name, take care of us. I–I thought it was the best thing to do."

Gaby looked at her arm, then at Bret, as though remembering giving the blood for the transfusion which saved his life in the Athens hospital. "And that's why I was a match– for Bret. I never...."

"And my blood wasn't a match." Heather had returned to the room, towel in hand, but her purpose in getting it apparently forgotten. She glared through tears at her father. "And you knew why, but hadn't shared that bit of information with me!"

Bret held both hands out toward his adopted daughter. "I didn't know about Gaby. That I was her father, I mean. I didn't know. I pray that someday both of you can forgive me, too."

"He didn't know, Heather. I didn't tell him. Don't break his heart, please. You are his daughter, in every way that counts."

Suddenly Dana could sit still no longer. She went to her daughter and knelt in front of her. "Say something, please, Gaby. I'd have cut off my arm before I'd hurt you. I felt I couldn't deprive you of your father figure. Only now I had to– and I have to hurt you more. I am so, so sorry."

Gaby looked confused, whispered, "More?"

"Heather, honey." Bret said, leaning toward her. "I didn't know about Susan's lifestyle when I agreed to marry her. But I can't regret it. I wouldn't have had you, the wonderful daughter who brought so much joy to my life. You've been my life. My reason for living." He paused, swallowed. "The rest of the story indirectly affects you, too."

"Can whatever it is be worse than what we already know now? God, what has happened to our lives, Dad?"

Dana sat on the sofa next to Gaby, still holding her hand. "This concerns your–Tod Pennington, too. It was so shocking to me, I could hardly credit it. But Sergeant McAlester assures me there is proof. I–I don't know how I can ever forgive myself for never suspecting."

"Mom, you're scaring me. What did–Dad, Tod, do that was shocking? He was an ordinary businessman, wasn't he?"

"No. He–he and the company were deeply involved in sex trafficking." Dana's face twisted in pain. "Even before we married."

Gaby sat motionless, a stunned look on her face. "No-o." She whispered. "McAlester must be wrong."

Suddenly both she and Heather swung toward Jon. An expression of sorrow filled his eyes as he looked from one person to the next. "Yes," he said softly, "I knew. I couldn't bring myself to tell you, even if I'd had a chance. But I knew it would have to come out."

"All this time, while you worked for me, you knew?" Bret's voice lashed out.

"No, not all of it. I only knew exactly what Susan was involved in for the last three weeks. I am sorry, Bret. You and Dana were so happy these last months. I couldn't lay all that sordid story on your happiness just before the wedding."

"And then Susan is killed immediately after we're married. Can there be a connection? Oh, God, surely not." Dana said.

Chapter Nineteen

Heather's phone trilled into the silence and they all jumped. She looked at the display. "It's Mona, calling from Lady Veronica. I'd better take it."

She stood up and walked into the foyer. The rest of the group could hear the murmur of her voice, but couldn't distinguish her words. After only a couple of minutes she returned to the living room. "I'm to meet her at the offices in Athens tomorrow at eleven a.m. She didn't say what it was about, but she sounded–different."

"I'm sure it isn't about you, baby. Probably a last-minute glitch in some publicity campaign." Bret said.

"Maybe." Heather didn't sound convinced. "Dad, I checked with Keira last night to see if Gaby and I could stay at the company condo until we went to the airport. She cut me off before I finished asking, said 'no' and then hung up on me. Something's going on."

Bret turned to Jon. "Is the helicopter still at the hangar in Lily Springs?"

"Yes. Shall I fly Heather to Athens?"

"Us. I'm going with her." He looked at Dana. "Do you mind, darling? I hate to leave you, but I'd really like to be with Heather since she feels something is wrong."

"Of course you do. Go. You'll be back before evening?"

"Surely. I'll call you when we're ready to start back."

Sudden realization spread across Dana's face as she turned toward Gaby. "Your internship! You're supposed to be in Nashville tomorrow."

Gaby was already shaking her head. "I can't leave you with all this. I'm going to call and leave a message and also text the firm right now. It's a family emergency. Surely they'll understand. If not, I'll find another internship."

"Honey. You wanted that internship badly. I'll be okay with Bret, Jon and Heather."

"I'm staying and that's that, Mom. "She squeezed her mother's arm and stood, pulling her phone from a pocket.

Next morning Dana watched her husband's Lexus pull out of the farmhouse driveway, Heather in the front passenger seat, Jon in the rear. Gaby came to stand beside her, handed her a cup of coffee. "We'll soon be swimming in this stuff, if we keep up our consumption."

"Yes. I'll brew some tea in a minute. We can switch up."

"I think I saw a bottle of that raspberry syrup you like in your tea up at the house."

"I think there is one there. I could go and get it later."

"No, I'll run up and get it." Gaby sighed and went to sit on one of the matching sofas near the fireplace.

"Mom. I don't think you and Bret told us all that Sergeant McAlester told you about–Dad. Damn. I can't seem to call him Tod, Dad, or anything else." She set her cup down, a little more forcefully than necessary.

"Honey. Of course, I understand. Whatever faults he had, and it appears he had many, he was there for you when you were growing up."

"Is there more?"

"Yes. They–the authorities are trying to determine who could have been Heather's biological father. Tod is one of the possibilities, obviously. And It's possible, of course, whoever he is has no bearing on her mother's murder."

"Which he couldn't, if it was him. But they won't know until they identify the guy." Gaby nodded. "Do they have any clues at all?"

"Hardly any. She gave Jon some hints that she may have tried to blackmail him and decided it was too dangerous. That's when she inveigled Bret to marry her, convincing him he was the father."

"The more we hear about the woman, the worse she sounds. Poor Heather."

"Yes. I'm sure she's feeling very conflicted. And now this with her employer. I hope it isn't anything serious." Dana reached for her daughter's hand. "Honey, you really didn't need to stay and babysit me. Maybe you could still meet the people at the DC law firm. Have you heard back from them?"

"Mom. It's okay. They said to get in touch with them again when the crisis is resolved. There might still be a possibility for the intern position."

"Oh, I hope so. I don't want you to lose that chance."

"There'll be others. Maybe even better. Don't worry, Mom. Now, is there any more the detective told you?"

Dana stared at the floor, her arms crossed, clearly reluctant to repeat what McAlester had told her and Bret. Gaby waited.

"I was sure it was a mistake. How could I not know my husband was in such a despicable business? For years." She dashed a hand across her eyes. "He showed me paperwork. Pictures on his phone of financial paperwork with descriptions of why the transactions were made, who was involved. I recognized Tod's signature."

Gaby asked, "Can you—can you just sort of generally describe what some of the transactions were about? You don't have to go into graphic detail, if there were any."

Dana answered, voice controlled, wooden. "I'll try." She took a deep breath. "One I remember, a big party at a hotel, this one was in Carbindale, I even wanted to go, sort of. But he said I wouldn't enjoy it. The paper detailed how thirty girls were provided for 'entertainment.' The girls were supplied with 'protection' and miniature recorders, suitable evening wear clothing." Her voice trailed off and she put her hands over her face.

"I'm sorry, Mom. That's enough. I get the idea. And he was doing 'business' like that all through my childhood, teen years, high school?"

"It seems so." Dana replied, misery in her voice. "I've—I've read a little and heard some news reports about things like that. They even use underage girls. And he had a young daughter."

Gaby's voice was stony. "Or maybe he didn't really think of me as his daughter. After all—"

"Oh, honey. I always thought he did." Tears of pain flooded Dana's eyes.

"There's something else you don't know." Gaby walked to the fireplace and fiddled with a ceramic figure of a cow. "I was researching which college would be best for my undergrad law school track, sitting at my computer. He came up behind me, put his hands on my shoulders and remarked that as a lawyer, it would take years before I'd make any money.

"I said I knew that, but it was what I wanted to do. Then he said some of the smart and attractive girls my age in his company already made six figure incomes."

"Oh. My God! Gaby! Do you think he actually had the idea of getting you involved in that sordid business?"

"I don't know. I told him I was quite sure I didn't want to do anything else but become a lawyer. He didn't say anything else and left my room."

"Baby, baby. I am so sorry. I can't bear it. To think..." Dana broke down, sobbing.

Gaby rushed to her and they wept together over years of deception by someone whose love and integrity they'd never doubted, until now.

Chapter Twenty

When Jon set the Kenyon helicopter down on the helipad atop the black marble-faced Lady Veronica building in Athens, one man waited near the rooftop entrance. Heather and Bret ducked under the whirling blades and walked toward him.

When they were close enough Heather spoke, "Phil, will this take long? Should our pilot wait or come back for us?"

"He should probably wait, Heather. I don't think this will take long." Phil shuffled his feet, seeming a little nervous. "They're waiting in the conference room with the company attorney."

"The company attorney? What is this about then? My contract isn't up for renewal for six months."

He wouldn't meet her eyes. "Ah, I'm sure they'll fill you in. We'd better go down now." He led the way to the elevator leading from the rooftop.

Three minutes later Phil opened the massive teak doors to the large conference room on the second floor. He followed Heather and Bret into the room. Bret knew the large, opulent room was intended to give them a feeling of insignificance. Phil closed the doors and went to a chair on the far side of the table.

Dave Fontenburg and Netria, his wife, sat together at the head of the table. Heather knew normally they sat at opposite ends. Dave did not rise at their entrance and Netria's stony gaze never left Heather. Dave waved a hand at two empty chairs across from the company lawyer and Phil, and ordered them, there was no other word for it, to sit.

"Dave. Netria. I'm a little confused. I thought this was–"

"It really doesn't matter what you thought, Heather," Netria's voice was as cold as her expression. "Since Silas Vail, our attorney, is here, you probably can guess this meeting has to do with your contract as signature model with Lady Veronica Cosmetics."

"Oh. Okay. Though it isn't due for–" Heather's reply was bluntly cut off.

"We do know when your contract expires. But we are terminating it early, for cause." Netria's hard black eyes bored into Heather's blue ones.

"Just exactly what do you mean, for cause?" Bret demanded.

Phil remained silent. Netria turned on Bret. "The contract which your daughter signed contains a clause that should she bring embarrassment to or besmirch Lady Veronica's reputation, her employment may be terminated by the company without recourse."

"What the hell are you talking about?" Bret exploded. "My daughter has never caused the slightest blemish on Lady Veronica's reputation."

Without comment the attorney pushed a copy of the day's Atlanta newspaper across the table. Heather's lovely face stared up at them. Beside her picture was another one, which appeared to be an older Heather. Below it was the word, 'Mother,' and below Heather's, the word, 'Daughter.' Heather seemed frozen, staring down at the pictures. Bret snatched up the paper, scanned the article.

"You can't terminate Heather's contract because her biological mother has been killed. She certainly didn't do it."

"Ah, in fact, we can, Mr. Kenyon. Such notoriety is not the kind of publicity a company like Lady Veronica needs to deal with." The attorney spoke for the first time.

"My God, this is the most cruel treatment of an employee I can imagine by a supposedly ethical company." Bret slammed the paper on the table.

"You are entitled to your opinion, Mr. Kenyon. But Mr. and Mrs. Fontenburg have to do what is best for their company." He slid a sheet of paper with the company letterhead across the table to Heather. "After you sign this acknowledgment attesting that you have been given a notice of separation, you will exit the premises, Ms. Kenyon."

Bret pushed the sheet of paper back toward the attorney. "She will not sign your damn paper. We most certainly will exit the premises. But you will be hearing from her and our attorney."

He shoved his chair back so hard it fell over. "Let's go, honey. This farce of a meeting is over." He looked at Dave Fortenburg. "Do you have no say when your wife and company attorney decide to commit dirty tricks?"

Dave's face held no expression.

Netria rose from her chair. "Get out. Phil, escort them and make damn sure that helicopter never lands on this building again."

Phil followed them to the elevator and entered with them. Bret's arm was around Heather's shaking shoulders, his mouth a straight line. He slammed his fist onto the silvery square marked 'Roof' inset into the wall of the elevator.

"Heather. I'm so..." Before Phil could finish the word Bret shot such a look of black fury in his direction his lips snapped closed.

When they emerged through the rooftop doorway Jon jumped down the steps, "That was quick..." he began as they neared the helicopter. His words trailed off as he saw Heather's tears.

"What happened?"

"I'm fired!" Heather managed to get the two words out, and climbed into the chopper. She turned her face to the window, chin quivering.

"Say what? Fired? Why?" Jon followed them into the chopper.

"We'll explain when we're in the air, Jon. Please just get us off this roof." Bret said.

Jon belted himself into his seat and started punching buttons and flipping switches. The engine whined as the blades whirled faster and faster and the helicopter rose smoothly into the air.

Bret had donned his headset and when they were at cruising altitude he spoke to Jon. "Request permission to land at Charlie Brown, please. I want to talk to that police Detective Sergeant if he's available. After I text him, I'll explain what happened."

He sent a text to Jud McAlester, asking to meet with him in forty-five minutes. When there was no immediate answer, he touched Heather's arm, said, "Sweetie, we'll fight this. You didn't do anything."

"Thanks, Dad." She half-turned, tried to give a watery smile, then turned back to the window.

He caught Jon's eye in a small mirror above the windscreen and spoke into his headset's mouthpiece. "The Atlanta paper ran a lurid story today about Susan's murder, complete with Susan's and Heather's pictures, side by side."

"Damn." Jon replied. "Is that why they fired her? How can they do that?"

"They used a clause in her contract about bringing unfavorable publicity to the company."

"But she didn't' do it!" Jon protested.

"Damn right. We're going to fight it."

"How did the paper get those details of the story?"

Bret's phone dinged with an incoming message. "That's what I'm going to find out from that Detective Sergeant. I can't believe the police department released that much information. Just a minute, he's answered."

He read the brief text and swore softly. "He's out of town. Won't be back until tomorrow. Says no info on how the newspaper got the story."

"They have a leak." Jon's voice was clipped. "I'd find out who, if I were him."

"So would I." Bret said. "So we'll go back to the farm. I'll call my law firm from there. Hopefully one of the attorneys has experience in this type case. If not, we can get a recommendation for one who does."

Heather spoke up, voice gaining firmness. "After this I don't want to ever work for them again."

"Sure, honey. But they need to be held accountable for this breach of contract. If nothing else, a big settlement should get their attention."

She shrugged. "Maybe I should take up some other line of work. Something useful like Gaby."

"If you want to consider getting out, you know I'll support you in whatever you do. But don't even think being a lawyer is necessarily better than modeling." Bret patted her arm, drew her into a hug.

"That's how I found you, Heather. After you won that trip to New York. I'm damn glad you were into modeling. Sorry to butt in." Jon said through their headsets.

"No apology necessary, Jon." Bret said.

Heather gave him a brief smile. "And I'm so very glad you did, too."

Chapter Twenty-One

Bret stood at his desk in his office back at the farm. Something kept nagging his mind. He couldn't quite put his finger on it. He thought it was something about the Lady Veronica meeting. The lawyer? Phil? One of the executive owners? He shook his head, better leave it alone. It would probably come back to him.

A light knock sounded on the door frame and Dana stepped in. "What are you shaking your head about, Bret? Besides the obvious, of course."

He walked toward her, took her in his arms and kissed her. "The Lady Veronica situation. But let's think about us for a few minutes." He led her to the settee under the double windows and they sat. "Are you sorry I came back into your life? Please don't give up on us. We'll get through this together."

"Certainly not sorry you're back in my life." She caressed his face gently. "I'm glad you know Gaby's your daughter. But I am so sorry if the truth hurt Heather. She's your daughter, too, even if not from your loins."

He turned his face and kissed her palm. "I am glad. I'm sure Heather is, too. She always wanted a little sister. It was just a shock."

He pulled her closer and she clung to him, laid her head on his shoulder close to his neck. "She wants a DNA test."

Dana raised her head, a puzzled look on her face. "What purpose would that serve? Aside from verifying her kinship to Jon?"

"I know. With no one specific to compare the results to, it couldn't tell her who is her father." Even as he spoke, he felt that little itch in his brain again. Was it some clue he didn't know he possessed that might lead to Heather's biological father?

She felt a faint stiffening in his posture. "Don't be hurt, sweetheart. You are the father in her heart."

"I know." He said again. "Not that. I can't bear to think she might be hurt again–if she found him."

"Like Gaby, when I told her–. But she will someday, soon be glad to know you're her father instead of...."

"And we'll be a happy family with our two beautiful daughters." He held her tight against his body and they sat quietly for a moment.

Heather's voice sounded from the doorway. "Sorry. I didn't mean to interrupt." She started to back away into the hall.

Bret and Dana both stood and held out an arm. "You're not interrupting. Come in, Heather."

She walked over and they pulled her into their embrace. Her eyes were still red and a little swollen. Dana's eyes reflected some alarm that Heather had not bothered to try and cover up the evidence of her tears. Most women, and especially a model, would have done that.

"I got a recommendation from my law firm for a lawyer who specializes in contract disputes in the public relations field." Bret told his daughter.

"I'm really not sure I want to do that, Dad. If they don't want me..." Her voice trailed off and she blinked back threatened tears.

"Well, I think you should sue the pants off them." Gaby declared. She stood framed in the doorway, arms crossed.

"Come on in, Gaby. Maybe a family caucus is in order." Bret beckoned for her to come closer.

Gaby walked over and joined the group, hugging Heather. "That Indian bitch and her silver-haired non-entity husband who never opens his mouth need a lesson."

"Let's sit." Bret invited. He and Dana took the settee again, Heather and Gaby the two matching upholstered chairs. "You sounded as though your dislike of the owners goes back further than what happened today, Gaby."

She frowned. "It does. I can't stand them. Though, of course, if they hadn't shafted Heather, I'd keep it to myself."

"Appreciate it." Heather gave a small grin.

"But what's the root of your dislike?" Bret asked.

Gaby crossed slim ankles. "They seemed nice, the day we were in Athens to see Heather named their signature model. All kissy, happy, happy. All one big family and all. But it was only for the benefit of the hundred press representatives who were there."

"And?" Bret pressed. "I don't mean to interrogate you, but it might be important."

"Well, early in the spring, I had a few free days and Lady Veronica was doing that big cosmetics trade show over in Memphis. I asked Heather if she might be able to get me a pass, so I could come backstage to say hello. She told me you couldn't make it so she did get the pass for me and I went. I saw first-hand how they treated some of the contract models. Netria would rip into them if one eyelash was not perfect. And Dave was there, too, but never said a word to tone her down. Just ogled the most beautiful girls."

Heather was nodding, an anguished look on her face. When Gaby paused, she said, "That's the way it was at all the shows. I felt bad for them. I tried to be friendly to them, but Netria didn't really want me to mingle with the other models. Said, 'They're not on your scale, ignore them.'"

"Do you know the names of any of those contract models? It might be helpful for the attorney to have them." Bret looked at Heather.

"I could probably get some. My agency handled some of them."

Bret turned back to Gaby. "So you think the woman owner, Netria, is the boss of the outfit?"

"Sure seemed that way. Heather?"

"Yes, always. But I never gave it much thought. I just figured they thought a woman could handle the models better. Which I didn't think was the case, like Gaby. And the owner/manager of my agency is a man."

Gaby stood up. "I'm going to do some more internet research on the company. And all the executives. Hang in there, Heather."

"I think I'll take a shower. Wash that place right out of my hair, so to speak."

Both girls left the room and there was silence for a moment.

Dana had a thoughtful look on her face. "I don't want to sound like a copy cat. But my first day back, the day you came to my house last year, Bret. And Jon flew us to Athens when they chose Heather. I sensed an odd feeling from the woman, Netria."

"What kind of feeling did it come across as?"

"Just a sort of impression. Like a secret animosity toward Heather she tried hard to keep hidden." Dana reached up to remove one of her silver earrings. "I don't know why I put these clip earrings on, I know they're going to hurt." She tossed it from hand to hand.

A shiver of something like recognition hit Bret and he sat very still. There it was, the key to the thing he'd been trying to remember. Come on, show yourself. His face must have shown his struggle to remember.

Dana leaned toward him. "What is it? Is something hurting?"

He blinked. "Uh, no. Let me see your ear." He pulled her dark wavy hair away from the ear nearest to him. He traced its contour.

"Bret. Why this sudden interest in my ear?"

"Not really yours, honey. Heather's ear. And the owner, Dave. His ear. Something I've been trying to bring out of my brain the last little while."

Dana waved her hand in front of his face. "Uh, Bret. You're not making any sense. What in the world can this Dave person's ear have to do with Heather?"

"Probably, God, I hope—nothing. Oh God, I really hope nothing." He replied. "But why do they both have it?"

"Have what? What, Bret?"

"A bump. On top of her ear, makes the top a bit thicker than the rest of the ear. Doctors offered to remove it. But she doesn't want any kind of surgery on her body."

They both jerked toward the doorway when Heather's voice spoke again. "I leave the room for a minute and come back to find you talking about my deformed ear."

She wore a white towel, turban-like, covering her long, blonde hair and a matching fluffy terrycloth robe.

"Oh, well. It is one of your more endearing characteristics, honey." Bret tried to laugh, but his voice sounded a little strained.

"You never could lie well, Daddy. And that's one of your more endearing qualities, right, Dana? Why don't you want to tell me why you were talking about my ear?"

"It will sound a little stupid, probably, baby. It's nothing."

Heather crossed her arms and tapped her foot, a picture of waiting.

"It is stupid. No possible connection. But–your boss, Dave?"

"Uh huh. Supposedly. He hardly ever spoke to me."

"This morning. I was watching him pretty closely, to see if he had anything to say, if he agreed with his wife."

"Okay." She nodded.

"He had those huge, gaudy diamond studs in his ears. I wasn't really thinking about it, just the thought crossed my mind that it kept people from noticing the top of his right ear, which was sort of–lumpy looking."

Heather dropped suddenly into the chair she'd occupied earlier. The color had drained from her face. She whispered, "Like mine."

"But it can't mean anything. Just coincidence. Has to be. There are probably thousands of people with ears like that."

"No, Dad. Different kinds of deformities of ears, not like mine." She smiled weakly. "And the crazy thing is, I'd noticed it myself. And just shrugged it off without thinking much about it. But that was before…"

"Before the accident." Bret went to kneel in front of Heather. "Baby, I know I should have told you. I know it."

She laid her head against his. The towel slipped sideways but she ignored it. "It's all right, Daddy. I love you. You'll always be my Daddy."

The three were silent for several minutes. Heather raised her head and sniffled. "Please say you understand, but I do want to have my DNA tested. Now especially."

Bret rocked back on his heels. "Your DNA? But, honey, why? What would be the point?"

She just looked at him as though waiting for him to figure it out.

After a moment, he said, "There'd be no way to get his DNA profile, Heather. And no way to compel him to give it."

"Whose DNA? What have I missed?" Gaby stepped back into the office.

The three already there glanced at each other. Heather answered. "Mine. I want to have my DNA profiled." She held up a tiny bottle with liquid in it. "Saliva." And a hairbrush with a number of blonde hairs in the bristles. "Hair."

Gaby's lips twitched. "You're serious."

"Very. If none of you will help me I'll find out how to get it done and do it myself."

"Baby. If you're determined, we'll help. Gaby, you must know how to go about it?" Bret rose, one knee creaking slightly, and stood beside Heather's chair, one hand on her shoulder.

"There are companies, laboratories, that specialize in DNA profiles." Gaby came into the room and sat down. She nodded toward the items in Heather's hands. "Yes, hair, saliva, those are things they would analyze. But they'll have sterile containers, sterile enclosed cheek swabs, et cetera. I know of one lab. Your attorney will want to check out others, I'm sure."

"Can't we just get it done ourselves?" Heather asked.

"You can. But it's advisable to do it through your attorney." Gaby paused, thinking. "As a matter of fact, I think I'll have mine profiled."

Suddenly it seemed as though all the air had left the room in a vacuum, and she looked up. Seeing the stunned looks on her mother's and Bret's faces, a guilt-stricken expression appeared on hers.

She rushed to her mother's side. "Mom, Mom, I'm sorry. I didn't mean to imply that you lied to me–us."

"I'm sure you didn't, honey. It just took me by surprise."

"Can you understand the reason I want to? So I can see in numbers and graphs that Tod Pennington is not my father?"

"Of course. With all that's come out, I can't blame you."

Just then a rift low on the horizon opened in the overcast clouds and a ray of sunlight speared through the window. When it touched one of Heather's crystal trophies won in a beauty contest, brilliant sparkles moved over their faces.

The sudden golden light seemed to energize Dana. "I think we should start putting some dinner on the table. Bret, your housekeeper came this morning and left a supply of dishes in the refrigerator and freezer. I'll start it. Where is Jon?"

"Probably down at his house. I'll call him to come up." Bret pulled out his phone.

Chapter Twenty-Two

Jon arrived just as Dana, Gaby and Heather placed the last dishes of vegetables on the table. Everyone took their places at the table and after Bret asked the blessing the bowls were passed around. Conversation was sporadic, as a subject that wouldn't cause pain was hard to come by.

When they had settled in the living room after dinner, Bret said, "Jon, we should fill you in on something Heather plans to do."

"About Lady Veronica?" Jon said, turning to Heather.

"No." Heather replied. "I'm going to have a profile of my DNA run by a genetics lab."

Her eyes widened when she saw hurt in his eyes before he looked down. "Jon, I'm sorry. It's not because of you. It's–something else I'd rather not discuss right now."

"I haven't gone down that road, but it's something I should do. Susan never told me, if she even knew, who my father was. Maybe I'll have mine run, too. Think they'd give a family discount?"

Everyone tried to smile, but it was half-hearted. "I know. That was lame." Jon added.

A moment later, he asked, "What lab are you thinking of using?"

"We're not sure. Gaby knows of one. Our attorney is going to check out some others, then we'll choose whichever he thinks is best."

* * *

Back at his house after dinner, Jon made coffee and pondered what their DNA results might tell them. A knock on his front door interrupted. He put the coffee carafe down and holding the cup he'd just filled padded on bare feet to answer the door. After opening it he stared in stupefaction at the blonde thirty-something woman who stood there. Hot coffee dripped on a bare foot as his hand tilted, unnoticed.

"Oww." He quickly righted the cup and tried to find words. "Uh, hello." It was the best he could do.

"Hello." The woman replied, smiling uncertainly. "Could you, maybe, be my brother?"

"Uh, uh. I think–I–uh–I think I might be." He opened the door wider. "Do you–want to come in?"

The woman stepped inside, looked around. Her eyes widened when she saw the glass cases of model planes and helicopters.

"Would you like a cup of coffee?" Jon asked, indicating his cup.

"No, thanks. You're Jon Blessing, right?"

He couldn't take his eyes from the woman, a lovely, but more mature version of Heather. "I'm sorry for staring. What's your name? Oh, and please, have a seat."

She sat at the end of the sofa and clasped a tote bag with a cat design in her lap. "I'm Willa . Willa North Younger. From South Carolina."

Jon's yellow tabby wandered in from the kitchen. He sat down in the doorway and looked at the newcomer for a minute. Then he rose and walked over to the sofa and rubbed the woman's ankles, finally put his front paws on the edge of the cushion and jumped lightly into her lap.

"Creek! No, get down." Jon started toward the sofa, but she waved him back.

"It's okay. I love cats." She smiled and pointed toward her tote bag. "Unusual name for a cat though."

"I found him on a creek bank, half-starved and half-frozen, trying to subdue a baby rattler. I finally enticed him to come home with me."

To gain time to compose himself, Jon took his cup to the kitchen and put it in the sink. He came back and sat down in a straight chair. "Why did you ask if I might be your brother." His gut told him he was indeed her brother. But innate caution bade him go slow.

"A few months ago I went through a rather acrimonious divorce. My mother and I umm–always had our own problems. But she liked my husband."

"Go on."

"During one of our arguments he told me something my mother had told him at some point."

"I'm sorry you didn't get along with her - them. What did he tell you she said?"

"That I was one of a set of twins, a boy and girl. But she and dad only wanted a girl. Actually she only wanted a girl. So they only took me."

"Had you suspected you were adopted?" Jon asked.

"Oh, I always knew I was. But not that I had a twin brother somewhere. Still, I kind of always felt - incomplete."

Jon was nodding, eyes never leaving her face.

"You felt it, too?" Her own searching gaze met his.

"Yes, I did." He whispered. "But my parents told me I was a twin. And why they only got me. They said..." His voice trailed away, not wishing to cause her more pain.

Her face crumpled a little, immediately guessing what he had been about to say. "Would they have taken both of us?"

"Yes." He moved to the sofa from the straight chair. Took her hand. "You've found me now. Don't look back."

She blinked rapidly. "I'll try. Your parents are gone?"

"Train wreck. When I was eighteen. They were good people. I'm sorry yours were - lacking."

"Oh, Dad was good, just weak. Mom ruled our home. She's - not well now, lives in an assisted living facility."

"Do you have children?" He asked.

"A son, thirteen. My pride and joy." Her face lit up when she mentioned her son. She pulled out her phone. "Here's his picture."

Jon gazed at a blond young man, holding a baseball bat and glove. A younger version of himself. He whispered, "My nephew."

She looked toward the glass cases of model planes. "He collects those, too."

Jon's face lit up. "Any aspirations to be a pilot?"

"Actually, yes." She replied. "Jon, did you - did you ever look for me?" Her eyes pleaded for an affirmative answer.

"If you only knew how hard I've searched. Hired private investigators. I only found our..." He broke off. Did she know about Susan?

"Our mother? Yes, I know she's been murdered. The news stories are how I found you." She twisted the handles of her bag. "What a terrible thing, that she had to be murdered for us to find each other."

"Please believe, I would have never stopped searching. So I suppose my picture was in the news articles?"

She nodded. "And her other daughter. Our younger sister. I've always felt so alone and now to think I have two siblings. It's kind of weird."

"I'll take you over to the main house and you can meet her." Then he glanced at the clock above the television set. "Maybe it's a little late. I'd better call first."

He started toward the kitchen to call on his landline. A large man stood in the doorway, a big gun in his hand. "No phone calls. Get over there with your sister." He waved the gun toward the sofa.

When Jon sat down again Creek stretched out a paw to touch his thigh. The man went to the front door and opened it. Another taller, thinner man came in. "Who the hell are you?" Jon demanded,

The big man walked over to him and slammed the gun barrel against Jon's temple. He fell against Willa. She shouted, "Why did you hit him? He wasn't doing anything."

Creek yowled and leapt from Willa's lap, raking claws across the man's ankle as he streaked for the kitchen. The man swore, swung his gun and fired toward the flying cat.

Willa screamed, "No." and launched herself from the couch.

The man shoved her back, growled, "Shut up or you're next."

Just then Jon's landline rang. After four rings the answering machine picked up. A woman's voice said, "Jon? I'm coming over, I need to ask you something. See you in a few minutes."

The big man swore. He ordered the second man, "Get the keys to his truck, drive it and meet us at our car. Douse the lights."

Jon moaned and sat up, holding his head. The man waved the gun at Willa . "You, help him to your car, passenger side, you're driving."

Jon's truck led the way, with one of the intruders driving, as the two vehicles drove the county roads, making a couple of turns. Through the pain in his head, Jon tried to remember the route they took. After about ten minutes they pulled into a driveway, drove around a sprawling one story house and into a large shed. Another car, a black sedan was already parked there.

The Stanhope place, Jon realized. The Stanhopes were on a month-long cruise, not due back for two weeks. These bastards must have known. And also known they could walk across the woods and fields between this place and Bret's without being seen. Since they had made no attempt to keep Jon and Willa from seeing their faces, he feared their intentions. He had to figure out a way for them to escape.

The man who had driven Jon's truck jerked open the passenger door and pulled Jon out. The back seat passenger got out and opened the driver's door. He ordered Willa , "Get out."

He shoved the two captives toward the back of the shed while his fellow kidnapper pulled the sliding door to the shed closed. The other joined them as the heavy-set man opened a door on the back wall. He took a flashlight from a shelf, switched it on and shone it into the small room, apparently used for junk storage.

"Kill that light. Sheriff's cruiser just drove by. Next time he'll stop and look around if he sticks to his schedule."

"Come here and close this damn door then. We'll wait until he does his thing and leaves before we go find a cell signal and report to–" He stopped speaking, then started again. "Find some rope, tie 'em up."

They found only a length of clothesline and tied Jon's and Willa 's hands together back to back on either side of a round post. Jon tried to hold his wrists in a way to leave a little slack. He wasn't too sure how successful he was.

The subordinate seeming man complained to the other, "Kidnapping two people wasn't part of the deal. Tell that to the bitch when you call her."

"You'd rather we'd stayed and it'd been three? Holding somebody against their will is the same as kidnapping, so shut your trap."

After they were secured the heavy-set man, apparently the leader, told the thinner man to slip back to the front and watch for the deputy. He returned after fifteen minutes, saying the deputy had stopped, gave a cursory look around, and drove away again. The two men left without another word.

Chapter Twenty-Three

As soon as he was sure they were gone Jon began flexing his wrists to try and slip from his bonds. But the clothesline was too tight.

Willa had not spoken since they arrived. "Willa, are you okay?"

He heard a faint sniffle. "Did I bring this on you?"

"Absolutely not. I think it was just their good luck, from their point of view, that you were at my house."

"But what do they want?"

He was quiet for a moment. "If I knew who they were working for, maybe I could make a guess."

"Do you have some idea then?" She tried to turn her head enough to see him, but couldn't.

He hesitated. Would it make her so fearful she would lose all hope of escape? "I wonder if..."

"Tell me, dammit." She spoke in a strong voice. "How can I help fight if I have no idea who I - we're up against?"

He smiled, in spite of their situation. Glad she had spirit. "I wonder if it might be the s.o.b. who's our sperm donor."

She gasped. "You believe he killed our - Susan?"

"Or had her killed. Okay, we need to get out of here before they come back."

"I'm for that. But how?"

"I have a small flat sharp-edged tool in my wallet. In my back jeans pocket. It's good this pole is round. Can you slide up it with me until we're standing?"

"I'll do my best. Let me draw my feet in. Tell me when to start."

Slowly and carefully they inched up the pole. About halfway, the line caught on a knothole which stuck out a fraction of an inch. Jon managed to get it past.

When they were on their feet, he moved his left hip to the side. "Now try and reach into my pocket and get my wallet.

Then we slide back down. Don't try and open it, just hold tight."

"Okay."

He felt her fingers trying to get into his pocket, slip. "If you feel embarrassed, shut it down. You can do this." Finally she reached his slim wallet and managed to extract it.

"Got it." She breathed.

"Great. Hold onto it. Ready? Slowly, slide back down."

Jon's legs were pretty shaky when they were again on the floor, he figured hers were, too. "All right. I'm going to take the wallet from you. I know where the tool is."

He carefully got the wallet, opened it somewhat awkwardly. He closed his eyes and his fingers inched open the flap to get the tool. He felt the edge slice his finger a little, but ignored it. He slowly manipulated the small flat blade until his thumb and index finger held it. Making tiny slices he sawed at the clothesline holding his wrists. After what seemed an eternity he felt it give way.

But a piece of line still bound Willa 's wrists to his. "Hold still. I'll try not to cut you, but can't guarantee it."

"Just do it, Jon. I'm more scared if they come back."

After another eternity he felt that line give and he was free. He turned to face the pole and cut her loose. When her hands were free she flung her arms around him.

He hugged her briefly and patted her shoulder. "I'll check the door."

He shoved at the door, but something heavy was hard against it on the other side. He put his shoulder against it as Willa joined him and together they were able to push it open enough to get out into the main part of the shed where his truck and her rental car sat.

They hurriedly checked both for keys, but didn't find them. They ran to the large main door and shoved it open on its sliding track. An sodium vapor security light shone on the left side of the building. Jon grabbed her hand and pulled her to the right just as a car's headlights turned into the driveway and started around the house. "Shit. No time to hot wire the truck."

The cone of light swept over Jon. He let go of Willa 's hand and gave her a little push. "Go. Hide in the woods."

She took off but shouted back, "Come on, Jon, come on, run!"

"I'll fake them out, then catch up. Go!"

He ran in an angle away from the direction Willa had gone, heard shouts. The beam of a flashlight stabbed the darkness ahead of him. A shot buzzed by his head. Too late he saw the drainage ditch in his path, pitched forward as another shot sounded. His forehead slammed into a large flat rock and all went dark.

Chapter Twenty-Four

Gaby stepped from her old professor's office to the main street of Lily Springs and looked around. For a Tuesday morning there was quite a bit of activity. She hadn't been there before so didn't know if that was normal for the small county seat. Diagonally across from her stood the stately historic courthouse. She could see if it was open for visitors.

But her mother was once a schoolgirl in the long brick building on the hill above town a couple of blocks away. It now housed a thriving indoor flea market, she'd been told by her old professor. Maybe she should check it out, since it would probably be years, if ever, before she had a chance again to see one of her mother's old haunts.

She decided to step just inside the entrance to the courthouse and take a quick peek at the lobby at least. A plaque next to the sidewalk said it was on the National List of historic places.

She returned to the sidewalk, walked past a ladies wear store next to a small art gallery and stopped at the curb of the next intersection. Someone grabbed her arm. Whirling, she tried to jerk loose, but the heavy-set man who held her was strong.

As she opened her mouth to scream, he spoke. "Drop the idea of suing Lady Veronica. It could be dangerous. You hear?"

"Who the hell are you? Let me go!"

"Pay attention or you'll wish you had." He hissed.

She did scream then, as loud as she could and dug her nails into his hand, drawing blood. He dropped her arm and walked rapidly away. A man leaving the ladies wear store ran to her, asking, "What happened?"

She pointed in the direction her attacker had gone, but there was no sign of him.

She pulled her shirt sleeve up and showed the man the imprint of fingers on her arm. "A man grabbed my arm, threatened me."

"What did he look like?"

Gaby was dialing 911 as she answered. "Big, heavy-set, thinning dark...hello, a man just grabbed me on Main Street," she looked at the street sign above her head, "and Rock Avenue. When I screamed he ran off." She listened a second, "Yes, I'm okay."

Several others had gathered to see what was going on. Gaby covered one ear in order to hear the dispatcher over the increasing noise. The man who came to her aid hurried back toward her, shaking his head. "Didn't see him anywhere."

"He does seem to be gone, a bystander ran to look for him but didn't see him. Okay, I'll wait here."

"She's sending police." Gaby told the bystander. "I'm Gaby Pennington."

"Yates Orton, County Attorney. Sure am sorry this happened to you in our town." The man, maybe in his middle forties with salt and pepper hair, put out his hand for a handshake.

Just then a Lily Springs Police car pulled to the curb and a uniformed officer got out, leaving the engine running.

He nodded to Orton, and looked at Gaby. "Ma'am? You called for police? Someone accosted you?"

"Yes. A heavy-set man grabbed my arm. When I screamed and scratched him he let go and left."

"Did he say anything to you?" The officer had his notebook out and wrote in it.

"He told me not to file a suit against a company I'm considering filing, that it could be dangerous."

The officer glanced from her to the County Attorney. "Are you an attorney?"

"No. I'm a law student." Out of the corner of her eye she saw interest flash across the County Attorney's face before it went bland again.

"What's the suit about?"

"A contract matter with a cosmetics company." Gaby said.

"Is the man who accosted you connected with the company?"

"I have no idea. I've never seen him before."

After Gaby had given the officer as much description as she could, he told her, "I'll put in a report and our officers will be on the lookout for this man." He looked at her hand.

Gaby followed his gaze and saw red stains on three of her fingernails. Since only clear polish covered her other nails, she knew it must be the blood she had drawn when she clawed the man.

"Would you be willing to come to the Forensics Lab at the County Sheriff's department a few blocks from here and let the Tech take a sample?"

"Sure," Gaby replied.

"I'll drive her over. My car is right here." Yates Orton pointed to a red jeep parked nearby.

"Hold on a second." The officer went to his car and took a package of plastic bags from the glove compartment. He handed one to Gaby. "Please put this over your hand until you arrive at the lab. Thank you, Mr. Orton."

"Let us know if you see him again." He tipped his hat to Gaby and the County Attorney, returned to his car and drove away.

Since the excitement, or lack of, was over the people who had gathered drifted away.

Orton led the way to his car and opened the passenger door. He pulled the seatbelt down so Gaby could fasten it with her left hand. When he was behind the wheel and headed down Rock Avenue he smiled and glanced over at her bagged hand. "Our worthy patrolman has aspirations for bigger things, I think."

"It would seem so." She smiled back.

After she had given samples from each nail to the tech on duty at the lab and washed her hands, Yates Orton took her back to the intersection. He parked and got out to open her door.

"Could I buy you a coffee, Ms. Pennington?" He asked, adding. "As an apology of sorts for this business?"

Gaby pointed. "Actually I was headed for the indoor flea market over there. And I'm still going." She started walking and he fell in with her.

"You know about our landmark? There's a nice coffee shop there, too. But you're not from Lily Springs, are you?"

"My mother is a native of the area. She was a student in the building when it was a school."

Orton nodded, a somber look crossed his face. "I thought I recognized the name. Dana Tucker Pennington Kenyon. I was with her in school there." He waved a hand at the building as they approached.

They entered through the original double doors, with small panes of glass which filled the top half of both. The floors inside were now tiled, rather than the oiled wood her mother had mentioned in years past. Gaby saw that some walls had been removed but some rooms still retained a classroom look.

Orton led the way down the main hallway and they entered what looked like two classrooms combined, a wide archway cut into the wall between them. The smell of fresh roast coffee drew them to the long serving counter.

When they had ordered they found a table against the wall and set their cups down. Orton pulled her chair out. "Car doors and chairs, too. A real Southern gentleman. Thank you." Gaby grinned.

He took his own seat and grinned back, which changed his face so he looked ten years younger. "I like the old Southern customs. One reason I've stayed in Sweetwater County."

"This is the first time I've been back since I was a baby. Aside from the wedding, I can't say it's been much of a pleasure." She set her cup down without drinking. "Sorry. But I'm afraid it's true."

"Hardly surprising. But speaking of the wedding, I realized who you were before you mentioned your mother was a student here. You were one of Dana's maids of honor."

Gaby caught the pensive note in his voice and hid a smile. It seemed Yates Orton had been another of her mother's youthful admirers. She wondered if she'd ever inspire that look in a man's eyes. Or had she glimpsed something similar in Sergeant Jud McAlester's expression once, in spite of Heather's vibrant presence beside her? She came back to the moment to realize Yates Orton had asked a question.

"I'm so sorry. My mind was somewhere else. What did you say?"

"Is there any progress in finding the person who killed the first Mrs. Kenyon?"

"Not a lot, I think. Although the lead detective investigating said they are 'pursuing some leads.'" She put air quotes around the last phrase.

He hesitated. "I don't want to sound like I'm interrogating you, Ms. Pennington. But I am naturally curious. Bret Kenyon's pilot was arrested and released, I understand."

"Call me Gaby."

"If you'll call me Yates." He smiled again, accentuating the cleft of his strong chin.

"Okay, Yates. Yes, Jon Blessing was a person of interest at first but his alibi was strong, so they let him go.'

Chapter Twenty-Five

Still in her pajamas and bathrobe Heather wandered into Bret's office, coffee cup in hand. "Good morning, Daddy."

Bret was just putting his phone down. "Morning, honey. The contract attorney Mitch recommends is out of town. He'll be back day after tomorrow."

"Did Gaby go to Lily Springs to see that professor she knew?"

"She left a few minutes ago. Mitch is also looking up the most reputable independent DNA labs. He'll call back."

"Thanks, Dad."

"You're sure that's what you want to do, baby?"

"Yes. I need to know. Even if..." Heather's face twisted in pain before she turned away.

"I'm so sorry you think there's a possibility - of that."

"I'm sorry that I hurt you by wanting the DNA done. I'm sure you've realized what the implications could be if..."

"Unfortunately, yes." Bret stood up and walked to the window. "If, unlikely as it seems, he is the one, we have to wonder did he know?"

"Gaby's digging into his background. And the company background."

"Did you ever hear how long Dave and Netria have been married?"

"No. The story went that she was a top model in India before they started the company. I heard snatches of gossip from a model who'd been with them several years. She said he always tried to put moves on some of the models. Especially blonde ones. She cut her eyes toward me when she said it."

"Sounds like he's something of an s.o.b." Bret said.

"Later another model pulled me aside and said not to pay any attention to her. That the other one had been in the running for signature model and what she said was sour grapes."

Dana tapped the door frame with the toe of her shoe and when Bret beckoned, came into the room. She was carrying two cups of coffee. She looked toward Heather. "I'm sorry I didn't know you with him, Heather." Handing one of the cups to Bret, she said, "Thought you might be ready for another."

Heather had moved to look through the window. She nodded to Dana. "Such a beautiful day. And we're all sunk in gloom." She turned back to the other two and flung out her hands. "This was supposed to be a wonderful, happy time for us."

"Sit down, baby, it will be. As soon as the police - learn all the facts we'll be able to get on with our lives."

"Will we? Who knows when we'll find out to whose sperm Jon and I owe our existence?" Bitterness touched Heather's voice.

Dana was looking at her husband. She saw the wince he tried to suppress and laid her hand on his. She mouthed, "I love you."

Heather had turned back to the window. "I know I must be the most selfish young woman in the world. Please forgive me, Daddy. You've given me a dream life and you must feel like I'm throwing it in your face."

Bret got up and moved swiftly toward his daughter. He folded her in his arms. "Never. I will never think that of you. When you hurt, I hurt. If you need to know who's responsible for your physical existence, I will move heaven and earth to find out for you."

"Thank you, Daddy. I guess I'm a little afraid to find out even though I'm pushing to do it. But whatever we find out, you will always, always be my real Daddy."

"You better believe it." He kissed the top of her head.

"I think I'll take a walk. Maybe see what Jon's doing. Does he still work on those model airplanes?"

"Of course. He has hundreds now."

After Heather left the room, Bret and Dana took her place at the window, his arm around his wife's still trim waist.

He asked, "Where was Gaby off to earlier? I saw her truck go down the driveway."

"One of her undergrad professors lives in Lily Springs. She wanted to drive over to talk to him. He used to practice in Atlanta, but she couldn't remember for sure what his field of expertise was. She thought maybe public relations contract law, but it may have been literary contracts."

"I am so sorry our family troubles kept her from her interview. I do hope it won't disadvantage her." Bret rubbed her back and drew her closer.

"She wouldn't entertain the thought of leaving, you heard her. She feels protective of Heather."

He turned her to face him. "Tell me. You met the Fortenburgs. What do you think? Is it possible he's her biological father?"

She took time to think about it, closing her eyes to visualize the hectic scene a year ago at Lady Veronica headquarters. "I just don't know. I only saw them – him - for a few moments. And there was such a mob. You had a closer look, for a longer time yesterday, what do you think?"

He gramaced. "It wasn't that long. They and that lawyer laid that crap on us immediately. And then we left."

"Did Mitch think there's a chance the law would see that they were wrong in firing her?"

"He's a lawyer. He won't commit to an opinion until he sees the contract."

"You faxed it to him?"

"Yes. He may drive out later today."

"That police detective hasn't contacted us for what - two days? I'm surprised at that."

"Yeah. And I'd like to know what, if anything, they've found out about who leaked all that information to the newspaper."

"That reminds me, a woman called yesterday while you and Heather were gone. She asked to speak to Heather. I told her Heather wasn't available. Then she asked who I was and when I told her she wanted to know how Heather reacted to her biological mother's murder. I hung up."

"Reporter." Bret spat out the word.

"That's what I thouight, too."

Bret's phone rang, bringing them out of their reverie. He answered, but the conversation lasted only a few minutes. His facial expression was less than happy.

"Who was it?" Dana asked.

"Sergeant McAlester. He's coming out in a little while. Wants to talk to all of us again."

"Did he say what about? Is there new information?"

"No, and he didn't say. I'll call Jon, he wants to talk to him."

He punched in a number. When there was no answer, he tried another. Dana guessed he'd tried the landline at Jon's small house, then Jon's cell phone number. And apparently got no answer at either one.

"He must have had an errand. He usually lets me know when he leaves the property, though I've never required him to do it." He walked to the window and looked toward Jon's small house, invisible as it was on the other side of a slight rise in the terrain. "He always answers his cell, but it just went straight to voice mail."

"Maybe he's in a dead spot."

"Yeah. Though there aren't as many of those around here anymore."

"I was gone so long, I wouldn't know." Dana put her arm around his waist and laid her head against his shoulder. "Shall we grab a sandwich or bowl of soup before the Sergeant gets here?"

"Sure. Maybe Jon will get my message before he arrives."

"Will you tell the Sergeant about Lady Veronica's despicable action? Or does it matter?"

Bret nodded. "I don't know, but we'll tell him. He'd probably think it odd if we didn't."

"True."

"If he comes out I hope Mitch doesn't arrive until after McAlester leaves. I'd like to not give him any idea we think one of us needs a lawyer."

"Mitch isn't in criminal law though."

"True," Bret echoed.

They adjourned to the kitchen where they found Heather, now dressed, making a grilled cheese sandwich. "Thought I'd eat before going to Jon's house, I was a little hungry, but nothing much appealed to me." She said, swiping a paper towel across the counter and dropping it into the garbage can.

"Elsie left a big container of tomato soup. A bowl of it might go well with your sandwich, Heather." Dana touched her arm as she passed the girl on the way to the refrigerator.

She and Bret decided to have a sandwich with their soup. In a few minutes they joined Heather at the dining table. Bret carried the sandwiches and coffee and Dana two bowls of soup she'd just heated in the microwave.

"Honey, Sergeant McAlester will be here soon. He wants to talk to all of us." Bret said. "Can you postpone going to Jon's for an hour or so?"

"Oh, sure. Do you think they've found any new evidence, Dad?"

"He wouldn't say. And have you heard from Jon this morning? I've been trying to reach him by phone."

"So have I. You don't know where he went?"

"No. He didn't mention needing to go anywhere today."

Heather lifted a spoonful of soup then spilled it back into her bowl. "Mitch hasn't called back with a recommendation for a DNA lab?"

Bret shook his head. "He's careful, you know. Wouldn't toss out a name lightly. Maybe he wants to discuss it."

Heather nodded. She dipped more soup, poured it back again. She stared unseeing toward the bay window which faced the fields. "Will there be a funeral before they find - her killer?"

"I don't know, honey, I don't even know who would handle things." He looked at Dana and asked, "Do you have any idea if any of her family are still around, honey?" He slapped his head. "God, darling, what a thoughtless thing to ask. Forgive me?"

"Of course, Bret. She was my friend, once upon a time. I thought so, anyway." She sighed. "But I've no idea if her sister and younger brother stayed in Rockvale or not. You remember her Dad died when we were still in high school. And her Mother soon after Susan graduated."

"I was in the city then, didn't buy this farm until I was sure I could swing it. You were almost seven, weren't you, Heather?"

She seemed not to hear him. "So unless my biological aunt or uncle is found, I'm the next of kin."

Bret cast a helpless look toward Dana, squared his shoulders. He covered Heather's hand with his. "We'll have to ask Mitch and Sergeant McAlester how that would play out, honey. Legally, it's probably a bit of a quagmire. When she abandoned us her parental rights were terminated. Then we found out I – couldn't be your biological father and I adopted you. So I'm not sure."

"So I might be looking at another legal battle if I wanted to claim her body and take care of funeral arrangements?"

Bret shrugged. "Maybe. Do you think you'd want to do that when the time comes?"

Heather was saved from answering immediately when the doorbell rang. Bret rose to go and let the visitor in. He returned to the table with Sergeant McAlester.

Chapter Twenty-Six

Dana asked, "Can we offer you a cup of coffee, Sergeant?"

"No, thanks. Hopefully I won't take up too much of your time." He sat in the chair Bret pulled out for him.

He looked around the table. "Are Ms. Pennington and Mr. Blessing around?"

"Gaby left a few hours ago. She'll surely be back soon or she would call." Dana explained.

Bret said, "Apparently Jon has gone somewhere, also. We've tried his land line and his cell phone, but he doesn't answer either one."

"All right." McAlester nodded. "Mr. Kenyon, do you or your daughter know if the brother and sister of Mrs. Kenyon are still in the state? We've not been able to locate either."

"We were just discussing that before you came. But no, we have no idea where they might be." Bret said.

McAlester looked at Dana. "You and the first Mrs. Kenyon were once friends. Do you have any idea about her siblings' whereabouts?"

Dana shook her head. "No. I've not heard of either for more than twenty-five years."

"It was a long shot." McAlester agreed. "But we haven't been able to find either of them. Another long shot. Do either of you know of any reason they would want to drop out of sight?"

"Seriously? They were an average small town family. Mr. Kent was a factory worker, before he died. The factory closed a year or so after I left Rockvale." Bret said.

"Was the mother employed? How did the family live after he died?"

"Truthfully, I don't know. Insurance and government assistance maybe?"

"Mrs. Kenyon?" McAlester looked at Dana.

She shrugged. "Neither do I. I know Susan - worked part-time. But I suppose they would still have been eligible for assistance."

"We've found the record of her mother's death after Susan graduated from high school. And her sister was in your class, I believe? She married shortly after graduation and we're checking Social Security records for her. But we didn't find a record for the younger brother. We're assuming he dropped out of school, related to finances, maybe."

"I suppose." Bret nodded. "She never mentioned either of them while we were together in Atlanta."

"So he didn't go to live with her? Which would seem the logical thing to do."

"So is her sister still in Rockvale?" Heather spoke for the first time.

"No. After she married they moved out west one person told us. Then dropped out of sight, at least we've not found her yet."

Heather looked at her father. "So I guess I am it, if she's to have a decent burial."

"That was a subject I was hesitant to bring up, Ms. Kenyon. The coroner has not released the body yet, but we wondered who to notify to take possession when he did."

"I will." Heather said firmly.

"We will." Bret said at the same time, gaze on his wife, imploring her understanding.

"Both of you, do what you must. Heather, I'm certain you would not want your birth mother buried in potters field. We'll get through it. If only..." she looked at Sergeant McAlester.

He seemed to understand her unspoken question. "We will find her killer, Mrs. Kenyon. It may take some time."

"You'd still like to talk to Jon?" Bret asked. When McAlester nodded, Bret pulled out his phone and tried both Jon's numbers again. When there was still no answer, a look of concern etched itself across his forehead. "He's never out-of-touch this long. I'm beginning to be worried."

"I'll be on my way then. Would you have him call me when he returns?"

Bret walked the detective to the door. Just as McAlester reached his car in the turnaround, a beige Lexus pulled in behind him. Gaby's truck pulled in behind the Lexus. McAlester spoke to both drivers for a few moments, then got into his vehicle and left.

"What did Sergeant McAlester have to say? Are they any closer to finding Susan's killer?" Gaby asked as Bret held the door open. Perry Mitchell, the Lexus driver and Bret's attorney, waved Gaby ahead of him.

"No, apparently not. You and Mitch introduced yourselves outside?" Bret asked. She nodded and he continued, "Was your old professor helpful?"

"No. His specialty was literary rights, not contract disputes." She answered over her shoulder and walked toward the living room. She looked around the group and went to sit beside her mother on the sofa.

Bret and Mitch followed and Mitch greeted Dana and Heather.

"Mitch, we'll go into my office to talk. Come on, Heather"

Gaby didn't expect they'd be long, lawyers seldom tarried when it wasn't necessary. The three were only in Bret's office about fifteen minutes before they came out and Perry Mitchell departed.

Gaby waited until Bret and Heather were seated again to speak. "Something happened to me in Lily Springs that's puzzling."

"Are you all right? What was it?" Alarm tinged her mother's voice.

"I'm fine." She sighed, and pulled up her sleeve. The bruises from the finger marks were even more pronounced now. Dana gasped.

"I'm fine," Gaby repeated. "A man grabbed my arm as I was walking down Main Street and ordered me to drop any idea of suing Lady Veronica. He left in a hurry when I screamed and dug my nails into his hand."

"You reported it?" Bret asked.

"Yes. A city policeman made a report. And the Sheriff's Department lab took samples from under my fingernails.

Looks like this family is going to be on every police blotter in this part of the state." She tried for some levity, but the response from her listeners was half-hearted.

"Oh, and I met the county attorney, Yates Orton. He was nice, kept apologizing for what happened."

"I hadn't seen Yates for many years until the wedding. Maybe he's matured since high school. I don't think Bret was too happy he came to the wedding." Dana gave her husband a fond look.

Bret half-smiled, "The guy never married. I didn't mind him as a guest until I saw the hungry look he gave you. Not that I blame him. You were, and are, a delicious sight to behold."

Dana blushed a little and shook her head. Then she asked, "Should we notify Sergeant McAlester about Gaby's attack?"

"Probably. I'll call him." He pulled out his cell phone and left a voice mail message for the detective, giving a description of Gaby's attacker.

When he finished he paced the length of the room for a moment, then walked to the window.

"I'm going over to Jon's house." He finally said, "I'm getting worried. Especially after Gaby's experience in Lily Springs."

"I'll go with you, Dad. I'm getting worried, too."

"Shall we all go? Mom and I are concerned about him, too." Gaby said.

"Maybe you two should stay here in case he calls." Bret replied. "Or, God forbid, somebody else with news of him."

They somewhat reluctantly agreed.

He and Heather walked outside. "We could take the golf cart, but maybe we should use the SUV."

"Surely he's okay. But why haven't we heard from him?" Heather fretted.

"Yeah. Sure hope he's okay."

Chapter Twenty-Seven

Five minutes later Bret pulled up in front of the old farm tenant house he'd remodeled into a comfortable home for Jon. Jon's well-kept old truck was not under the carport but his car was, a newer mid-size Suburu.

Bret led the way to the front door and knocked, not expecting an answer. Silence reigned inside and outside for half a minute. Bret knocked again and a sudden noise, like running footsteps sounded inside the house.

Bret already had his key in hand. He stepped to the side, pushed Heather behind him and quickly inserted the key and turned it. Waited. They heard the sound of a loud bang, like a door slamming hard against a wall. Bret shoved the front door open, reached inside and flipped a light switch. Seeing no one, he pulled Heather inside with him. He pointed toward the sofa on their left.

"Get behind that while I check out the house. Careful of the glass."

She ducked behind the floral printed sofa and whispered, "Dad, be careful."

He nodded, put his finger to his lips. The door to Jon's bedroom was ajar. Trying to avoid the shards of glass from broken display cases of model airplanes, he walked toward the bedroom door. No sound came from the room. He stood to the side of the doorway and quickly pushed the door inward as Heather watched from the end of the sofa. When there was no reaction he looked inside, saw no one and let out the breath he didn't realize he was holding. He stepped to the closet and checked that it also held no one.

He quickly backtracked to the living room, checked that Heather was still behind the sofa and crunched toward the kitchen. He felt a breeze and knew the back door was open. Whoever had been here must have left when he knocked. He went over and closed and locked the door. Only then did he notice that the kitchen had been as messily searched as the bedroom. Bags of sugar and flour had been dumped on the counter, drawers and cabinet doors hung open, boxes of staples flung haphazardly on the shelves.

Heather spoke behind him, "Why would someone search Jon's home? I looked in the bedroom, it's completely torn up."

"I have no idea. I'll call the county sheriff, then Dana. Don't touch anything else."

Heather retreated and stood by the front door. "I don't like this. I'm a little scared."

Bret patted her shoulder, then dialed 911. When the operator answered, he said, "I'm Bret Kenyon. I want to report a break-in at the tenant house on my farm." He listened for a second, then replied, "No, no one is hurt that I can see, but the place has been searched. My employee lives here, but he's not home. I've not been able to reach him so came to check."

Within half an hour a Sheriff's cruiser drove along the private road and parked on the side. A heavy-set deputy got out of the driver's side of the car and a thinner younger one emerged from the passenger side. They walked toward the small porch where Bret and Heather waited. Both deputies touched their hats and stood stiffly in front of them.

The heavier deputy seemed to hesitate, then offered his hand. Bret smiled briefly, "You don't have to be so formal, Chuck. You were at my wedding a few days ago."

The deputy shook hands vigorously, "Thanks, Bret. My wife was really excited when you and Mrs. Kenyon put that open invitation in the paper."

"Very glad you all came. I'm sure you both recognize my daughter, Heather." Bret couldn't keep a note of pride from his voice. He turned to the other deputy, who was trying not to stare at Heather. "And you're Hart Wilson, right, deputy? You were at my wedding, too, weren't you?"

The younger man nodded, "Yes, Mr. Kenyon. My daddy talked about you a lot before he died."

Bret nodded. "He was a good man."

Chuck Corbett spoke again, "Sheriff Glass will be here in a little while. He was up to Bremen when the call came through. Want to fill us in, Bret?"

"Sure. The man who lives here is my helicopter pilot. He was over at the house last night, left to come home around ten. My daughter and I have both tried to call him, on the phone here and his cell phone several times today but got no answer. I have a key, of course, so decided to come over and see if there was any clue where he'd gone."

"He usually let you know when he's going to leave?"

"Yes, as a courtesy in case I might need him. I don't require a certain number of hours from him."

"And you said the place had been searched?"

"It's a mess. There's a lot of glass from his display of model planes. After I knocked we heard a noise, then a few seconds later when I knocked again we heard a sound like a door slamming closed or against the wall. When we went in, I discovered the back door open. We must have interrupted the search."

Chuck looked at Hart, indicated he should look around the back. Deputy Wilson walked toward the corner of the house and out of sight.

Corbett walked to the other corner and disappeared from view. He returned a moment later. "Didn't flush him out. Probably long gone. Y'all stay here, I'll take a quick look around inside. Sheriff's picking up our forensics man."

"Okay, Chuck."

After his old friend went inside Bret called Dana again to update her and Gaby. Heather went to sit in the SUV, leaving the door open. Bret heard a plaintive 'meow' and looked down as a yellow tabby cat wound around his boots.

"Creek!" Heather cried as she jumped out of the car. "I didn't even think of him."

"Me, either. So Jon didn't mean to be away overnight, he'd have asked us to check on Creek."

Heather picked up the cat and nuzzled his fur. "He must be hungry. We should take him to the main house."

"Yeah. Though I doubt he's hungry. He lived in the wild for several months until Jon finally enticed him to be friends. He's missing Jon, probably."

Sheriff Glass arrived with a dark-haired deputy who carried a metal box, which he set down on the ground while the Sheriff talked to Bret. He nodded when the Sheriff introduced him, Raymond Forrest, and his light brown eyes held an admiring gleam when he looked at Heather. His gaze sharpened as he looked around the yard, taking in the row of deep pink blooming azalea bushes along the edge and carefully laid flagstone path to the front porch.

"Okay, Ray. Let's see if the intruder left any trace that might give us a clue who he is. Bret, you and your daughter can go back to your house. I'll stop by when we're done."

Glass turned to go inside, then looked at the cat Heather still held. "Inside cat?"

"Inside and outside, there's a pet opening on the back door." Bret replied.

Glass indicated the cat to Ray, who already had his case open and brought out a small brush. He went over to Heather and the cat. "Will he mind if I do a brush stroke to get some hairs?"

"He'll probably think you're petting him. He loves to be petted." She stroked Creek's head with a finger as Ray ran the brush down his back. Creek purred loudly.

"See?" Heather smiled.

Ray said, "I get along with most animals." He went back to his case and carefully placed the brush in an evidence bag then followed the Sheriff into the house.

"Ready?" Bret asked Heather, getting into the car. "We can't go inside and get his carrier so I guess you'll have to hold him."

"He'll be fine," she replied.

Chapter Twenty-Eight

They drove back to the farmhouse. Dana met them at the door, a question in her eyes. They softened when she saw the cat. "Hi, Creek. Was he inside the house?"

Bret kissed her as they entered "No. I guess he was hungry and since Jon wasn't there to hand out food he decided to go get dinner, or breakfast, himself."

"You don't think Jon was home all night."

"Couldn't really tell. His bed was tossed, mattress half on the floor, so couldn't tell if he'd slept in it last night or not."

"There was a cup in the sink, but no way to know if it was there before he came here yesterday or later." Heather said as she put Creek down on the floor. He immediately began exploring, sniffing along the baseboard. He'd been in the house before but not in the recent past. "I'll go put bowls down for his food and water.

Heather started toward the kitchen, Creek trotting after her. Gaby came into the foyer from the hall carrying her laptop.

"Jon not home?"

"No, and I'm worried. Someone searched his house."

Gaby's eyes widened. "And no clues to Jon's whereabouts? Or the identity of the intruder?"

"No. At least, not obviously. The Sheriff's forensics tech is going over Jon's house now."

"Think I'll get some water, too. Dad? Would you like a glass?"

"Yeah, I got a little warm while we waited outside. Unusual this early in April."

Just as Bret and Dana started to follow Heather to the kitchen, the doorbell gave a long peal. Before Bret could reach the door, it sounded again. He opened it, then stood rooted to the spot.

"Bret? Who is it?" Dana came to stand beside him. She exchanged a puzzled look with her husband, who had made no move to open the storm door.

Dana reached for the handle as the woman spoke to them through the glass. "Please. I'm sorry to bother you, but is this the Kenyon house?"

"Yes." Dana answered, opening the door and beckoning her to enter. "Come in. You look worn out. Have a seat."

The woman sank to the cushion on the antique wooden settee against the wall, still grasping her tote bag tightly. "I am. I've been hiding and walking for hours."

"Who are you?" Bret managed to get the question out.

"Here." Gaby had gone to the kitchen and returned with a glass of water, offering it to the woman. Heather followed her, staring at the newcomer. Creek ran past Heather and leapt into the woman's lap.

"Creek! You're okay. I was afraid they might have found and hurt you." She petted and hugged him, adding to the bemusement of the onlookers.

Heather finally gasped out a question. "Dana? Is this Susan's sister?"

"I don't think so." Dana replied. "Are you?". She asked the woman.

"No. I'll explain, but give me a minute, please, I'm parched." She took the glass from Gaby. "Thank you." She drank thirstily, paused and took another long drink.

She looked around the semi-circle of faces. "Is Jon here? Didn't he tell you?"

"Tell us what? How do you know Jon? Have you seen him?" Bret demanded.

The woman's face filled with fear as tears filled her eyes. "He's not here? Oh, God. They must have caught him. Call the police!"

"The Sheriff is at Jon's house. Were you there? Was it you that searched his house?"

Tears streamed down her dirt-streaked face and her hands shook. Gaby grabbed the glass. "We ran away. After two men kidnapped us. They left us tied up in a shed, but Jon managed to get us loose. He told me to run, that he'd catch up. But he never did."

"Who are you? Were you at his house?" Bret demanded again.

"I'm Willa, his sister. Oh, where is he? I just found him. They can't have killed him! Please, God." She pleaded.

Comprehension dawned on four faces.

"His twin. My half sister." Heather knelt and took the woman's hands. "Dad. That explains it."

"Explains?" Willa looked from one to the other.

"How much you look like me. And..."

"Her! Susan." Willa spat the words.

Bret and Dana exchanged a worried look. Bret asked, "Willa, how long have you been in Georgia?"

"I drove down from Charleston yesterday. Why?"

Bret looked relieved, but apprehension quickly returned. "We want to hear your story, but I think I better get the Sheriff over here. Are you hungry?"

"Starved. I've only had a couple of cookies I found in my tote bag."

"Honey, show her where to clean up, and give her some food while I call Calvin."

Dana nodded and held out her hand to help Willa up. "Come, there's a powder room just off the kitchen and we'll get some food in you."

"Thanks." Willa took Dana's hand and pulled herself to her feet. Creek moved over to lie on her cat print tote bag.

"Creek sure seems to have taken to you. I guess he met you at Jon's house?" Bret caught Dana's eye and shook his head in warning. "All right. Let's get that food," she continued briskly and led the way to the kitchen.

Willa barely had time to wolf down a sandwich of deli roast beef and cheese and a glass of tea before Sheriff Glass arrived.

He entered the dining room and took a seat across from her. He raked her with a sharp gaze. "You say you're Jon Blessing's sister? Do you know where he is?"

"I am his sister." She cried, tears threatening again. "Are you looking for him? Those two thugs must have caught him. I should have stayed, too."

"Name? Address?" Glass took out his phone and tapped keys.

"Willa North Younger. I live in Charleston, SC." Her hands clenched on the table as she strove for self control.

"Start from the beginning. Why are you here?"

She took a deep breath. "The Charleston newspaper and television stations carried the story about Susan Kenyon's murder. The TV news showed her picture and also one of the model daughter she'd abandoned as a baby. It showed a quick shot of a man who'd been questioned and released, Jon Blessing. I was adopted as a baby, but my adoptive parents didn't take my twin brother. The daughter looked so much like me and my son is the image of Jon. I had to find out if he was my brother."

"Why did you think he might be your twin brother?"

"I told you, my son looks exactly like him. I never knew I was a twin. My mother told my husband long before, but not me. She just wanted a girl, so the agency allowed them to take only me. I've looked for my brother ever since my husband let it slip about a year ago."

"So you saw the news story and immediately drove to Georgia?"

She swiped tears from her eyes. "Please, find him. I can't lose him again."

"We're searching, Mrs. Younger." The Sheriff said, not unkindly. "But I need you to tell me what happened at his house."

"I drove there. His phone number and address were in the directory, the GPS in my car took me to it. He was surprised, but he'd been searching for me, too, he said. I'd been there for about twenty minutes. He started to call here, he wanted me to meet Heather. A man came through the kitchen, he had a gun, and he let another man in the front door. He hit Jon with the gun, but it didn't knock him out. Then the phone rang, a woman said she was on her way to Jon's."

Heather gasped. "It was me. Oh, God."

Glass nodded. "We heard the message. Go on, Mrs. Younger."

"When he hit Jon, Creek jumped from my lap and scratched his leg. The man shot at Creek, but I'm so glad he didn't hit him."

"We found the bullet lodged in the wall. Continue, ma'am."

"They forced us into my car and the second man drove Jon's truck to a shed in back of a big house. They tied us up and left in their car to call someone to find out what to do with us. Jon got us loose and we were running away when they came back. He told me to run, he'd catch up with me, but they must have caught him." She bit her lip and her hands gripped each other so hard the knuckles were white.

"Did the men say why they came, what they wanted?"

"No. We asked, but they just told us to shut up."

The Sheriff's phone sounded a note. He looked down, seemed to read a text. He rose and went through the mudroom to the back door, touched a key and spoke a few words. He listened, turned to look at the group in the kitchen and returned.

"Sheriff?" Bret asked.

"Jon Blessing has been found. The good news is he's still alive, but he's badly injured. He was found in his car in a ravine on the east side of the county."

Bret, Heather and Willa all jumped to their feet. "Where is he?" Bret demanded.

"He was stabilized in the Lily Springs Hospital and transferred to Atlanta Regional. Still in critical condition."

"I have to see him." Willa cried. "Bret, will you take me to him?"

Glass was dialing his phone. "Hold on, people." After a moment he spoke into his phone. "Commander? Will you have a State Highway Patrol car meet us at the county line past Rockvale? And take over escort for some people to Atlanta Regional?" Another pause. "You heard. Thanks. Fifteen minutes."

"Thanks, Cal. Let's go, folks." Bret led them to the front door, looked around. "Where's Dana?"

"Here." Dana hurried toward them, carrying sweaters and a tote bag.

The Sheriff had gotten outside before them, the big engine of his cruiser already running. They walked quickly to the SUV and piled in. After they had belted in and Bret took off after the Sheriff, Dana handed the sweaters to the women in the back seat. "Hospitals are always cool." She passed the tote bag to Willa . "I grabbed one of Gaby's outfits and some personal items for you, Willa. After we see how Jon is you can change in a restroom."

Willa looked down at her torn and muddy clothes. "Oh, Lord. I forgot how I look."

"Well, I guess." Gaby said. "Mom, that was thoughtful of you."

After that there was silence in the vehicle as Bret pushed the big car over the blacktop, keeping up with the ululating wail from the Sheriff's siren.

The Sheriff pulled over and waved as the dark blue and white State car took over the lead at the county line.

Gaby finally spoke. "I am so sorry to be the one to say it. But we better pray. Jon must be in bad shape or they wouldn't be doing this."

"Do it, Gaby." Bret said.

They held hands. Dana reaching with her right hand over her shoulder to take Gaby's, her left resting on Bret's right shoulder and Heather pushing her hand past the side of the front seat to rest on her father's left shoulder. Willa in the middle held both girls's other hands.

"Lord God, we asked you to touch Jon Blessing with your healing light, guide the doctors as they treat him and bring him back to us. Amen."

"Amen." Everyone echoed.

"Thank you." Willa said softly. "How I have needed this, family that loves and sticks together. For me and my son."

"'We got you, babe.'" Gaby smiled as she paraphrased the old Sonny and Cher tune. "I needed it, too. Without even knowing."

"Oh, have you called him? Your son?" Dana turned her head toward the back seat so she could look into Willa's eyes.

"Yes. When I got near your house, I could get a signal. I didn't tell him what had happened. Just that I was checking in, I'd call him later."

Heather asked, "He knows why you're down here?"

"Yes. I told him everything. He wants to meet his uncle, my twin." Her voice broke a little on the last word.

"Not much longer." Bret said, staying on the State car's tail as traffic parted and pulled to the side before them. "I hope the Trooper stays with us, or the Atlanta PD picks us up." Bret said. "Speak of the devil. There's McAlester."

McAlester's dark sedan with its dash mounted blue light and siren pulsing took off from the curb as they entered the city limits. The trooper's cruiser slowed, siren falling silent. He saluted as they flashed by.

Chapter Twenty-Nine

Five minutes later they pulled up beside McAlester's car in the emergency parking area of Atlanta Regional hospital. He and Bret strode fast toward the entrance, the women almost trotting to keep up.

Dana, and she was sure so did Heather, fought a feeling of *deja vu* as they hurried to the triage desk.

McAlester spoke to the nurse who keyed her computer and answered. He turned back to the group. "Blessing's in surgery. We can go up to the surgical waiting room and when he can, the surgeon will come out and talk to you."

After an interminable elevator ride to the fifth floor, they emerged into a large waiting area, filled with people. "I'll let them know you're here." McAlester said, and started toward an information desk as they found seats.

Willa clutched the cat print tote bag in front of her body, the one Dana had given her hanging from her shoulder. Heather's left reached for Willa 's right hand and groped for Gaby's with her own right hand. They leaned close, as if drawing comfort from each other. Dana caught Bret's eye and they shared a loving look laced with apprehension.

A half-hour passed, another. McAlester left to call in, brought back coffee, left again. They sipped coffee and waited some more. Willa didn't want to leave the waiting room for fear of missing the surgeon. Dana went with her, after convincing her to change by saying she knew Willa wouldn't want to upset the injured Jon by her battered, muddy appearance. When she returned in Gaby's clothes and with minimal makeup she bore such a resemblance to Heather that several heads turned.

At last a tall man in green scrubs, large sweat stains under his armpits, came through double doors and walked toward them. "Blessing family?"

"Yes," Bret said. "How is he, doctor?"

"As well as we can do for him at the moment. He had a ruptured spleen, so extensive internal bleeding, plus a skull fracture. We stopped the bleeding and he's stable, but we'll have to wait until he wakes up to evaluate the effects of the skull fracture. He's in intensive care, one floor up. One of you at a time may go in for five minutes each hour. I'll be checking on him. Excuse me." He turned and left the room through the double doors.

The group hurried to the elevator and went up to the ICU waiting room. Dana knew Bret wanted to be first, but he deferred to Willa and led her to the desk beside the ICU entrance. The nurse pressed a button to open the door and Willa went through.

Five minutes later she returned, wiping tears. "He's still unconscious. Covered in bandages. I squeezed his hand and told him we were all out here pulling for him, that he's going to be fine." She swiped a hand over her eyes. "He has to be."

Sergeant McAlester came back into the waiting room, his eyes widened a little and he looked from Heather to Willa and back to Heather. They filled him in on Jon's condition.

"Do you want to go down to the cafeteria so we can talk? I have some information."

They agreed and followed him to the elevator. Willa was visibly torn between wanting information and staying near Jon, but went with them. They found an empty table in a corner and they gathered around it.

McAlester looked at Willa first. "The kidnappers were apparently in a hurry to leave the place where you were held after the shots were fired, in case someone heard them and called the Sheriff's office. They tried to clean up evidence but left a little of the line they used to tie you up. Sheriff Glass's men found your car in a ditch a few miles from the Stanhope farm, wiped clean. Jon seems to have stumbled and fallen over a drainage ditch. There was blood on a rock as though he'd hit his head. They dragged him back, put him in his truck and one of them drove it away, followed by the other in their vehicle. After they pushed the truck and Mr. Blessing into the ravine, they put yours in the ditch hightailed it to Rockvale to call their employer."

Bret asked. "There was enough evidence that they figured all that out?"

"Actually, no. One of the men got scared, and he doesn't fit the description of the man who accosted you in Lily Springs, Gaby - Ms. Pennington. He walked into State Patrol Headquarters and turned himself in. He wants a deal before he says anything else."

"A deal?" Bret slapped the table.

"Kidnapping and attempted murder, he's not apt to get much of a deal from the State's Attorney."

Gaby asked, "So they pushed Jon's truck off the road with him in it, already injured?"

"That's most likely the case. The guy who turned himself in claimed not to know for sure. He said he picked up the guy as he was walking along the road to get farther from the scene."

"Why?" Willa 's voice was filled with anguish.

"The witness doesn't know. Sheriff Glass, the State and the city of Atlanta detectives are all digging for evidence."

Bret narrowed his eyes. "Why the city? It happened in Sweetwater County."

"Thought you'd ask. Seems these two men have been involved in several cases in different states where strong-arm tactics were used."

"Criminal cases? Gang related? Underworld? Jon can't have been involved in something like that."

"Various. Most involving seemingly normal, upstanding business folks who thought force could solve their problems."

McAlester looked slowly around the table. "So what started all this?" He asked in a soft voice.

Heather's voice sounded strangled. "The murder of our birth mother."

"Seems so."

"And Lady Veronica fired you." Gaby added.

Willa spoke up, "And because of it, I found my brother."

Dana asked, "But how is all that a threat to somebody?"

"The threat is most likely the motive for her murder. And the rest were attempts to cover up." He looked from Gaby to Dana. "I don't mean to add to the pain of either of you. You know of your late husband's involvement in an unsavory business. Which also involved Susan Kent Kenyon. We believe there is a connection between that and her murder. We just have not uncovered it yet."

After hashing the facts around a little more, McAlester left to check out a lead and the rest of the group took the elevator back up to the sixth floor. In a few minutes Bret took his turn to go in and see Jon, promising Heather she could be next. When he came out again four pairs of female eyes sent a question to him. He shook his head, "No change. But his vitals are steady, the nurse said that was a good sign."

"Definitely," Dana murmured. She looked at Willa. "You still haven't eaten properly. Let's go back to the cafeteria and get some dinner. It's almost seven o'clock."

Bret and Heather decided to stay in the waiting room, requesting the three bring a snack for them when they returned.

Dana chose a vegetable plate from the steam table while Gaby and Willa picked up premixed salad bowls and packages of dressing. All three decided water was a good choice of beverage since they'd consumed so much coffee lately.

Though when they began to eat worry seemed to overpower their need for nourishment, and they mostly pushed the food around.

Finally Willa put down her fork and searched Dana's face. "Do they think that Jon might have been almost killed because I felt I had to come to Georgia?"

Dana put her hand on Willa's arm. "No, I'm sure they don't. I think we're all convinced that everything is connected to Susan's murder. Who knows, they might have killed Jon outright if you hadn't been there."

"Why do you think they might have?"

"You heard the one who turned himself in say kidnapping wasn't part of the deal. Certainly not of two people. Maybe they were just supposed to warn Jon to leave things alone." She paused. "Or stage an accident."

"You could be right, Mrs. Kenyon." A male voice said as the owner, Sergeant McAlester, appeared around a nearby partition. "May I join you? Again?"

"Of course." Dana replied.

McAlester sat across from Gaby. He nodded to the two other women but his gaze lingered just a second longer on her face. "We have new information. Do you think Mr. Kenyon would like to come down to hear it?"

"Yes. I'll text him." Dana pulled out her phone and quickly keyed in a message to Bret. He answered immediately that he'd be right down.

When he arrived at the table five minutes later Bret told them Heather would be down as soon as she saw Jon in just a few minutes. "She said go ahead and tell us and she'd hear it when she came down."

"Your Sheriff's investigator had a stroke of luck. Two actually. He was looking for evidence in an outside trash can at a burglarized house near Lily Springs. He found a throw-away phone. Back at his lab he found its call history had been wiped."

Bret frowned. "Sergeant, I'm confused. What does that have to do with any of this?"

"Maybe something. Sweetwater County's lab is a little more sophisticated than your average non-State lab. And as with most State labs, ours usually has a back log. So when area agencies around Sweetwater really need a quick basic report, they ask Sweetwater for a favor. When the suspected kidnapper turned himself in to the State Police he was very anxious that they take good care of his personal effects. Among them was a throw-away phone that turned out to be the same model as the one Evans, the Sweetwater investigator, found."

"And?" Bret prodded.

"They brought it to Evans at the Sweetwater lab to do a quick check and he found the two phones had consecutive serial numbers. The really lucky part is what happened when it rang. Evans answered and tried to be noncommittal, but the caller realized he wasn't the phone's owner and hung up."

McAlester paused and they waited in silence for him to continue.

"He ran a check on the caller's number. Turned out it belongs to an owner of the Lady Veronica Cosmetics company."

"Say what?" Bret exclaimed.

Heather arrived at that moment and they made room for her, pulling a chair from another table. "No change, I guess?" Bret asked.

She shook her head.

Willa asked McAlester. "So the man who turned himself in is one of the men who kidnapped us?"

"We believe so, Ms. Younger. We'll need you to identify him, probably tomorrow. That's not all. A phone in his possession was examined by the Sweetwater County Lab. There was blood trace on the phone." McAlester looked across the table at Gaby. "We'll check to see if it's from the man who assaulted you. I suppose it could be from broken glass at Blessing's house."

Bret leaned toward McAlester. "Have you identified him yet?"

"Not yet. The only fingerprints on either phone belong to the man in custody. He isn't talking yet. He says we need his information, but he's not going to say a word until he's assured of a deal."

"S.o.b." Gaby muttered.

McAlester raised his right eyebrow. "I agree. We and the State Attorney have some good interrogators. They'll get it out of him." He stood up from the table. "Right now my boss is insisting I'm due for some down time. I'll check with you all in the morning. I hope Mr. Blessing has a good night. The rest of you try and rest, too." Sergeant McAlester stood up and walked away with a last glance in Gaby's direction.

Dana did not miss the little interaction, but said nothing as they all left the cafeteria and went upstairs.

Chapter Thirty

As soon as they entered the ICU waiting area a nurse hurried over to them. "Mr. Blessing is waking up. He seems a little agitated. The doctor thinks if one of you is with him, perhaps it will help calm him, Mr. Kenyon."

Bret didn't hesitate. "Go, Willa." She gave him a look of pure gratitude and took off.

"His twin sister. She was with him and he saved her life the night they were attacked." Bret explained to the nurse.

"I see the resemblance between her and this other young woman. Another sibling?"

"They've just found each other, it's a complicated story." Bret's eyes were on the door to the ICU proper.

"I'm sorry. I don't mean to pry." The nurse hastened to apologize.

Bret waved it away. "It's fine. Unfortunately you'll be reading about it in the paper for days probably."

Someone across the room beckoned and the nurse seemed relieved to have a reason to walk away.

A long fifteen minutes later Willa returned, a tear stained but happy expression on her face. "He's awake. And aware. He was as relieved to see that I'm okay as I was to see him awake."

Heather went to her and they shared a joyful embrace. "Can he have any more visitors tonight?"

"He insisted he has to see everyone. The nurse said, two at a time for two minutes only and then he has to rest. And she means it."

"Dana, you and Gaby go, then Dad and I will be last." Heather shooed them toward the door.

After everyone had told him how happy they were to see him and bade Jon good night, they discussed going home.

"Willa and I are staying here. The rest of you go, get some sleep," Heather ordered.

"Bossy, huh? Way ahead of you, baby. I called and took a suite at the hotel just down the street. If you and Willa decide you want a bed later, just come on down." He gave them the suite number and key card then he, Dana and Gaby left the hospital and went to the hotel.

Around three a.m. Bret woke and lifted himself on his elbow in the king-size bed to admire the woman he'd loved so many years. He almost pinched his forearm, again, to convince himself she was at last his wife. He eased off the bed and emerged from the master bedroom into the living room of the suite.

As he started to the small kitchen he heard a muffled sound from the sofa near the window. He froze, and it came again. Someone was trying to stifle their sobs. Gaby. He turned toward the window, spoke softly so as not to startle her. "Gaby, sweetheart. Are you okay?"

"Oh. Bret, I'm sorry, I didn't want to disturb you and Mom."

He knelt in front of her, took her hand. In her other hand she clutched a sodden tissue. "You didn't. I wanted a drink of cold water. Do you want to talk about what's bothering you?"

"I'm not sure. I'm an adult. It shouldn't matter now."

A spear of alarm went through him. "Honey, is it bothering you that your mom and I married?"

She squeezed his hand. "Please, no. Don't think that for a minute. I am so happy for the both of you. You deserve your happiness."

"What, then?" His left knee creaked a little as he rose to sit on the sofa beside her.

She buried her face in her hands. "That name... He called me that name. She used it."

"Who used..." Then it hit him. Damn the woman. Was there no end to the trouble and pain she could cause, even in death?

"You mean the name Susan used? Susie Penny?"

"Yes. He knew you were my... It was his sick little inside joke. Unknown to Mom, he was taunting her."

Neither had heard Dana step to the bedroom doorway. But they heard her audible gasp.

Bret almost leapt across the room and caught her as she swayed and clutched the door frame. He carried her back to the sofa and sat beside Gaby, Dana on his lap, right arm tight around Gaby. Dana pulled Gaby close.

"My baby. I am so, so sorry. I hoped you wouldn't remember. You don't deserve any of this. I should have stayed at Cattail Farm to have you. Grandma and Grandpa would have welcomed you with much love."

Gaby kissed her mother's cheek. "Maybe. But you did what you thought best for me. I'm okay. And now I have my rightful Dad with my blood in his veins and not one, but two sisters. And a brother!"

Bret's face lit up. He looked from Gaby to Dana. "And if you're agreeable, if it's what both of you want, I'll adopt you, too, Gaby. And you can have your rightful name as well."

Her face shown. "You'd do that?"

"Adopt my own daughter? You better believe it."

The three sat in a happy huddle for ten minutes, saying little, enjoying each other's presence. Gaby suddenly gave a big yawn.

"To bed with you, daughter! Yesterday was one heck of a stressful day." Bret kissed her forehead.

Her happy smile would have lit up the city. "I think I'll be able to sleep now." She extricated herself from her parents embrace and stood up. Kissed Dana's cheek. "Goodnight, Mom." And Bret's forehead with slight shyness. "Goodnight, Dad."

With final hugs all around they sought their beds.

At seven-thirty Wednesday morning as they perused the room service menu, the door to the suite swung open. Heather and Willa tiptoed into the room. When she saw them sitting around the table in the small kitchen, Heather said, "Morning, all. We wanted to be quiet in case you weren't up yet."

"You're just in time to order breakfast. Or do you want to sleep first?" Dana asked.

"Food." The two newcomers chorused.

"The hospital food isn't bad, but four-star room service is bound to be better." Heather snatched the menu.

"Have you seen Jon this morning?" Bret asked.

"Yes, briefly." Willa sank into a chair. "He's more alert. Broken arm a little painful. He's already asking when he can start rehab on using it. If he'd lost its use because of not being found in time, I'd want to shoot the - um – sorry thugs." She growled.

"Makes two of us." Bret's hand clenched into a tight fist.

"Three. And I've never held a gun in my life." Heather said.

"I think we'd all have wanted to," Gaby agreed. "And I do have a carry permit and shoot at the range regularly."

Bret gave her a thumbs up. "We'll have to take Heather and let her see if she'd like target shooting."

"I like it And have my permit, too." Willa said. "Does Jon shoot, Bret?"

"He does. Crack shot. But I'm starving, let's order. We can't go out and hunt our breakfast as folks used to do."

Within half an hour a server rolled a loaded room service cart into the suite. Bret gave him a generous tip and as he left they were all lifting lids to sniff the delicious aromas. They transferred it to the table and fell to after the blessing. Willa had asked with some diffidence if she might give thanks, for the food and for her newfound family.

When they were all sufficiently nourished, Dana set her cup down and announced she was going to shower and dress. "I've lolled around in this fancy monogrammed hotel robe long enough." She chuckled.

"And if no one else wants it, I'll take the paper and catch up on the news. I haven't seen one since - for several days." No one commented on Bret's obvious change in what he meant to say.

After they had left the room, Heather caught Gaby's eye. "Do you remember I said I wanted to go through Susan's home?"

"Of course. But I'm still not sure it's a good idea."

"I still want to though. And Willa says she'd like to go along. You don't have to if you feel strongly enough about it."

Gaby shook her head. "I'll go. I can't say you'll be going against legal advice since I'm not a lawyer yet. I will say it's a little against my better judgment. But if you go, I'm going."

Heather reached and squeezed her hand. "Thank you."

"So what's the plan?"

"We're going to sleep a couple of hours. We napped at the hospital, but it wasn't very restful, as you can imagine."

"While the rest of us are at the hospital? Then what?"

"We'll come by, maybe see John. Then decide we want to go somewhere. Maybe shop for some more clothes. Which we do need to do."

"And when we come back without new clothes?" Gaby asked in a dry voice.

Heather shrugged. "Nothing suited us. Or we could make a quick stop at a boutique I know and grab some slacks and tops."

"Sounds like you have it all worked out. Okay, I'll get dressed and one of you can have the other bed in my bedroom. The third bedroom is all ready for the other."

* * *

When Bret, Dana and Gaby arrived in the ICU waiting room, Bret was allowed a few minutes to see Jon. He came through the doorway beaming.

"Good news?" Dana asked.

"Oh, yes. He's doing so much better he will be moved to a step-down unit within the hour. The nurse told him they need his bed for seriously sick folks even though he made their job much easier."

"That's wonderful." Gaby said. "What floor will he be on?"

"This same floor, but he'll probably only be there for a day or so if he keeps improving like he has, she said."

Dana said, "Willa will be so relieved. I wonder how long she'll stay in Georgia."

"After you all left the table, she said something about maybe having a friend bring her son down for a week, since he's on spring break from school."

"Jon would love that, get to see his nephew."

They all jumped when a woman's urgent sounding voice suddenly came through the loudspeakers, "Code Blue, sixth floor. Code Blue, sixth floor."

They exchanged scared looks. Running feet sounded in the hallway as techs and nurses rushed past the doorway, one shoving a cart with equipment on it. All was quiet after their passage and the buzz of conversation in the waiting room started again.

Fifteen minutes later the attendant at the desk came over to speak to them. "Mr. Blessing has been moved to the step-down unit. You can move to that waiting room and they'll let you know when you can see him."

"Thank you. You've been very good to keep us informed."

"You're welcome. I hope Mr. Blessing recovers quickly and completely."

Chapter Thirty-One

"We could check out Susan's house now, before we go to the hospital." Heather said as Willa joined her in the living room of the suite, yawning.

"Without Gaby?" Willa paused on her way to the kitchen.

"I made fresh coffee. How did you sleep?"

"Pretty well. Have you talked to the family? How's Jon?" She continued to the kitchenette and poured a cup of coffee. She held up the carafe, "Refill?"

"I'm good." Heather replied. "Jon is now ensconced in the step-down unit in another wing on the same floor."

"Thank you, God!" Willa said fervently.

"You said it." They slapped palms after Willa set her cup down on the table.

"So, should we? Go to Susan's before we go back to the hospital. It would save explanations, er - misinformation–which I've always tried to avoid with my Dad."

"I hear you. I don't like dishonesty. I've had a hard time forgiving my adopted mother for not telling me about my brother."

Heather gave her a sympathetic look. "Yeah. I guess I gave my dad a bit of a hard time for not telling me the truth. But his motive was good."

"Whereas Mama's motive was selfish. She knew it was wrong. She admitted she didn't want to have to explain leaving my twin brother behind."

"Are you avoiding answering my question? Or thinking about it?" Heather looked closely at her half-sister's face.

Willa sighed. "I'd like to avoid prevaricating, too. But also I don't want to hurt Gaby."

"I know. Me, either. What if we call her and see if she can think of a better story for us to be away from the hospital a couple of hours?"

"Put the burden on her, huh?" Willa replied.

But Heather was already dialing Gaby's number."

She walked to the window overlooking the street and pulled back the drapes. "Gaby, everything still okay at the hospital?"

She was silent for a moment as Gaby answered. "Where are you?"

"The elevator!" She walked toward the entrance. "Okay, opening door. Hey, Sis." They disconnected phones and hugged.

"Hey, you two." Gaby sauntered inside and closed the door. With a wink, she asked, "Are we ready to go shopping?"

"What did you tell Dana and Bret?" Willa asked.

"Thought you'd wonder. Mom gave me the perfect exit excuse."

"Oh?"

"She didn't bring any makeup or clean unmentionables either, of course. So we're to pick up a few things for her and ourselves. Even insisted I take her credit card and put everything on it."

"Bet Dad didn't hear her say that or he'd have made you take his." Heather laughed.

"Actually he did hear it. And wouldn't have it any way but that we use his."

"When I'm home he'll hardly let me buy a stick of gum. I asked how he expected me to grow up. He just waved it away."

"Well, I think you've both done them proud. I mean it." Willa slung her tote bag on her shoulder and linked an arm with each of the other girls.

"Thanks, Willa," Gaby said as they hurried to the elevator. "I can't help but notice that tote seems to mean a lot to you. You held onto it in your wandering around Sweetwater County."

"It does. It was the first gift my son bought for me with money he earned doing odd jobs around the neighborhood."

"That was sweet. No wonder you held onto it." Heather said.

When they reached the lobby, Heather halted on their way to the entrance. "Cab or rent a car?"

"Do you know anything about the area where Susan lived?" Gaby asked.

"A little. It's not in a really nice section of town." Heather frowned.

"Then how about we call that car service company and have the driver wait? But not a limo. It might stand out too much. I expect Da- Bret would prefer you, and we, be safe."

"You're right." She touched Gaby's arm. "I don't mind you calling him 'Dad', Gaby. He is, after all."

"Thanks. It just, you know, still seems a little new and strange."

"Hmmm. You comforted me, steered us through the adult adoption process last year when he adopted me. Why can't he adopt you, too?"

"Actually, he can. And says he's going to do it."

Heather squealed. "That is so wonderful. I should have known." She threw her arms around Gaby. They reached out and pulled Willa into the group hug.

"OK. That's settled. Times wasting. Let me call the car service." Heather pulled out her phone.

Ten minutes later a sleek black sedan pulled up in front of the hotel. They piled in and gave the driver the address. His expression turned doubtful. "Are you sure that's where you want to go, ladies?"

"Yes." Heather replied. "We want you to wait for us. We won't be long."

When the car turned down the street that was their destination, they saw why the driver had objected. The buildings were run down, trash piled on some of the steps, overflowing garbage cans in front of others.

The driver pulled into a parking space in front of a four-story building at the address Heather had given. This one was marginally better-kept than most of the others on the block, but paint peeled from the steps and the railing on one side was hanging loose.

"I'm not sure you all should enter that building." The driver said. "If I may say so."

"Thank you for your concern. My - mother lives here. We want to look at her place." Heather added, "But don't go anywhere."

They got out and walked up the steps, careful not to touch the railing.

At the entrance they hesitantly pushed the door open. The smell of hot cooking grease and others they didn't care to characterize assailed them.

"I can't understand why she lived here. She was supposed to be a high-priced – hmmm - escort, I guess you could say." Heather was the first to voice their thoughts.

"I'm glad it's on the first floor. I'd just as soon not go up those stairs." Gaby said. There was an elevator but an 'out-of-order' sign was taped on the door.

Heather led the way as they approached apartment five and the other two bumped into her as she stopped suddenly. They peered around her and saw why she had halted. The door was splintered around the knob though pulled partly closed. Yellow tape hung from one side of the door frame and puddled on the floor.

"Not good." Gaby muttered. She clutched her purse, one hand in a pocket on the side. She hadn't mentioned to the others that she was carrying her handgun. She didn't think it would freak Willa out, but it might possibly have Heather.

She pushed Heather gently aside and moved ahead of her. "Against the wall." She whispered and demonstrated. Then reached out and pushed the door further open with her boot. Nothing happened so she pushed harder. It went back against the inside wall and bounced back a little. Still no sound from inside the apartment. She motioned for the others to stay back and entered, looked quickly from side to side, barely registering the condition of the room.

As she started to turn and motion the others in, she saw they were just behind her. Heather gasped. "Just like Jon's place. Surely the police didn't do this."

Gaby had her weapon out now, said "Stay here. I'll check the other rooms."

Chapter Thirty-Two

The apartment was small, only one bedroom and a small kitchen, both in the same condition as the living room they had entered.

She returned to the others, looked at Heather. "So what can you expect to understand from this? If there was anything of interest, whoever did this most likely found it."

Heather's expression was determined. "I still want to look around. They might not have found whatever they were looking for."

"Okay. Ten minutes. I'll stay near the door and look around, you do whatever you need to. Willa? Do you want to look, too?"

Willa whispered, "Yes. Just a little. She was my birth mother, too."

Heather first checked the small bathroom between the kitchen area and bedroom. It, too, had been searched. Make up was a puddle in the sink, bath powder covered the counter like snow. Tubes of lipstick lay everywhere, something sharp had been jabbed into each one and red streaks decorated the walls. It almost looked like blood and she shivered.

A small box that had held tampons lay in the corner between the sink and wall. Several tampons were scattered around it. Without thinking she picked up one of the cylindrical cardboard objects. Odd. It felt faintly heavier than the cotton formed into a similar shape inside should feel. She pulled on the string which protruded slightly from one end. An inch or so of cotton came out with the string and a metallic object dropped to the floor. She stared at it. Her mother, presumably, had hidden a flash drive in one of her tampons. She started to pick it up, paused in the act, tore off a few squares of toilet paper and wrapped cardboard, tampon piece and flash drive in it.

In the bedroom Willa ran her fingers along the top of the door frame, scowling at the dirt they picked up. All the drawers of the dresser and night stand had been pulled out and upended. The mattress on the single bed had been turned over, slit from top to bottom as had the box spring.

She picked her way to the single small window and looked out on the junk strewn alley. One end of the curtain rod hung down, the flimsy curtain dragging the floor. Automatically she picked up the rod to put it back in its bracket when something rattled in it. She shook it and nothing happened. She shook it again, harder. A small object fell out and bounced underneath the bed frame. When she reached underneath the footboard to retrieve it, she felt something taped to the bottom edge, pulled it loose. A flash drive.

Gaby called from the living room, "Heather, Willa, I think we'd better go."

Heather and Willa walked out of the bedroom, dazed looks on their faces. Heather whispered, "We did find something. Three somethings. Call Sergeant McAlester."

A shadow moved just outside the apartment door. Gaby saw Heather's gaze change direction and whirled, bringing her gun up. A figure moved quickly down the dark hallway and through the outside door. She backed further into the room, weapon pointed toward the door as she handed her cell phone to Willa. "Speed dial four."

Only ten minutes later Jud McAlester's car pulled to the curb in front of the building and the siren wound down. But faint blue light continued to illuminate the dark hallway with intermittent flashes through the outside door. They heaved sighs of relief when he entered the apartment, his own weapon drawn.

"May I ask why you three are in this apartment?" He speared each with a sharp look and did not appear happy to see them.

Heather stepped forward. "I wanted to see my mo - my birth mother's home. I thought I might spot something..."

"That the police missed?" He turned to Gaby, a scowl on his face. "And you went along with this?"

"Yes. I was party to it." She admitted.

"We all were." Willa declared.

"Aren't you going to ask if I have a permit?" Gaby couldn't keep a bit of anger from her voice. Her gun was pointed at the floor now. They could have been attacked and she might have been forced to shoot someone.

"I'm aware you do. You can put it back in your purse or holster, or wherever you keep it now."

Willa looked at their angry faces and jumped in, probably to avoid further acrimony, Gaby thought. "And we did find something."

"What, pray tell?"

Heather held out her hand with the tampon and flash drive wrapped in paper. "I'm the only one who touched it."

Willa held her hand out. She'd found a scrap of cloth and the flash drives she'd found lay on it. "Three somethings, actually."

McAlester stared at the objects in their hands. "I'm surprised none of you can pick a lock." He looked at Gaby. "Did you bust in the door? And did you have to tear up the place to find these?"

"We didn't do it, Sergeant. It was like this when we got here. But Heather wanted to look around anyway." Gaby said in an even voice.

"Okay. Don't touch anything else. I need to get these in an evidence bag. Ms. Kenyon, Ms. Younger, hold on to them and please come with me." He glanced at Gaby. "You stay here." He led Heather and Willa out to his car and they all returned in a couple of minutes. McAlester now held the flash drives in three clear plastic bags with labels. "We'll need all your fingerprints. I'll get Forensics in here - again."

When he'd made the call, he asked, "How did you get here? Cab?"

The three women exchanged puzzled looks. "No, we used the car service. We told the driver to wait out front."

McAlester shook his head. "There's no car service outside."

"What? He said he'd wait." Heather exclaimed.

"Did he come in here with you?"

"No-o-o. At least we didn't see him."

"You sound as though you saw something."

"When we came out of the bedroom after finding the flash drives to show them to Gaby, I caught movement out in the hall. Then someone ran out the entrance. That's when we called you."

"Gaby?" If he noticed he'd used her first name, he ignored it. "Did you see this person?"

"Just a dark figure as it went through the doorway."

Within ten minutes the apartment seemed filled with men, two in uniform, another detective in a suit, the others in casual clothing, white shirts and dark pants. The three women were requested to go over their stories again, separately, outside. As they passed through the hallway faces peered from partly opened doorways.

The other detective questioned Gaby in a green Ford that had seen better days. McAlester had introduced him as Detective Don Black. "So you were closest to the doorway, but you didn't get a good enough look at the person who left to be able to identify him?"

"No, Detective. I only saw the back of a dark figure."

He nodded. "I understand. But a person notices some details without realizing it. For instance, was he, if it was a he, as tall as the doorway?"

Gaby thought for a minutes. "I see what you mean. No, but there wasn't much clearance. Just a guess, six-eight inches, maybe. And I have an impression of thinness."

"Clothing?"

"Dark. That's all I can say."

"You're doing good. Shirt loose, tucked in? Tight against the body?"

Gaby's eyes widened. "Not a shirt, I think. But something seemed to catch for just a second on the side of the door. Jacket?"

"What do you think?" His sharp eyes searched her face.

"I think it was. A jacket."

Black looked past Gaby and nodded again. The passenger door opened and Jud McAlester asked, "Finished?"

McAlester held the door for Gaby as she got out and they stood on the sidewalk.

Black came around the car and joined them. "She saw a little more than she thought. Dark clothing, maybe a loose jacket, possibly six-two or three, he cleared the door by about six or eight inches. It's seven feet high."

"Good. One question. Could it have been the driver of the car you arrived in?"

She considered. "I didn't see him except sitting in the car. I don't know."

McAlester and Black exchanged glances. McAlester asked, "He didn't get out and open the car door for you? Either when he picked you all up or here?"

"No-o-o, now that I think about it. Not usual, is it?"

"Not usual. We'll check on the driver." Heather and Willa had joined them.

"Now, I'll take you three wherever you want to go. Hospital?"

"Actually, we need to do some shopping. None of us brought any extra clothes and we're getting a little ripe."

He smiled. "I hadn't noticed. I'll drop you in the downtown area then. Black, I'll drop the flash drives at the lab, and see you back at the station in about half an hour."

"We all finished in there?" Detective Black indicated the building.

"Yeah, the techs will secure the place when they leave." Black got back under the wheel of his car and drove away.

"We can take a cab, Sergeant. No need for you to take us downtown."

"I don't want you waiting around this area for a cab." Gaby and Willa frowned and started to protest further. "Don't get your backs up. I know you can take care of yourselves. But I don't want Bret Kenyon on my case if you even had to."

Heather shrugged. "He has a point. Why not?" She walked to McAlester's car and climbed in the back seat. Willa followed her inside.

Gaby started to get in the back also but McAlester said, "A little snug with all of you in the back. One of you can sit in front."

Willa turned to Heather and winked, whispered, "Good timing."

When they were all buckled in McAlester asked, "Any place downtown you prefer?"

"Yes, please." Heather answered, and gave the address.

"I talked to your father earlier." Gaby turned her head sharply, but he was looking in the rear view mirror, speaking to Heather. "He said Jon Blessing had been moved from ICU."

"Thankfully." Heather and Willa said at the same time.

"I'm glad. Anything else come back to you, Ms. Younger, that might help us identify the main attacker?"

"I'm afraid not, Sergeant. I wish." Willa replied.

"If he was involved in the search of Susan Kenyon's apartment, maybe we'll get lucky and find a fingerprint. Or there'll be something on the flash drives to help identify him."

McAlester double parked to let them out in front of the boutique. They got out and thanked him for the ride.

"You're welcome. But I hope you all will think twice, and call me, if you get any other bright ideas. One of the very least favorite duties of the police department is informing parents when something happens to their offspring."

"We are properly chastised, Sergeant." Heather answered. "Thanks again."

She led the way into the small elegant store as McAlester pulled back into traffic.

Anxious to get back to the hospital they made quick work of choosing, with Heather's expert guidance, outfits for themselves and one for Dana. A few other necessities and in twenty minutes they hailed a cab to return to the hospital.

"Heather, I can't believe you bullied me into allowing your dad to pay for my things!" Willa repeated for the third time.

"Enough already. Call it a 'welcome to the family' gift." Heather squeezed Willa's arm.

The muscular female cab driver glanced at the packages on the passenger seat. She grinned and said, "Hey, need any more family members, I'm available."

"At least it wouldn't take a death in the family to discover you." Gaby said.

"Oh, I'm sorry. I didn't mean anything by what I said."

Gaby flipped a hand. "It's fine. Don't worry about it. It was a strange remark from me. It's been kind of a roller coaster week for us."

The cab rolled under the covered entrance to the hospital. The driver said, "Well, here we are. I hope whoever is sick gets better real soon."

"Thank you. Stay safe on the streets." Heather handed the driver a roll of bills as Willa took a couple of the bags.

Eyes wide, the driver said, "This is too much." And tried to hand some of the bills back.

"Nope. Keep it." Heather waved it away and grabbed the rest of the packages. She hurried after Gaby and Heather into the hospital lobby.

Chapter Thirty-Three

Wednesday Afternoon

Dave Fontenburg entered his wife's office on the fifth floor of Lady Veronica's headquarters. He threw a stack of public relations printouts from modeling agencies on her desk. "None of these are going to do. We'll never find a signature model the caliber of Heather Kenyon."

"So you think." Netria sneered. She lit a pencil-thin foul-smelling cigar and blew smoke toward him.

"I do think. Have you even looked at these cows?"

"What you think is that I don't know about all of your fooling around. I've only overlooked it to keep up the company's reputation."

"And have you conveniently forgotten where I found you? Where would you be today without me?"

"Better, I'm sure, you prick. I may be over the hill as far as modeling, but I'm not stupid."

He laughed heartily. "Modeling. You could call it that. You looked good in those leather thongs, sure. But that was then."

"You bastard." She jumped to her feet, leaned over the desk and thrust the cigar at him. "You were happy to take the makeup formulas I'd worked out to set up this business."

"And it was my business sense that made you a fortune. Remember that." He shot back.

She screamed, "For which you thought the perks included jumping every model who appealed to you."

"Earned rewards, my dear. I never pretended to be something I wasn't with you."

He sighed, picked up the pack of pictures. "A CEO's work is never done. I'll interview some more of these. Maybe I'll get lucky and one will be half-way suitable."

"Get lucky?" She screamed. The door had barely closed behind him when the ashtray she hurled struck it.

Back in his own office, his phone rang as Dave was in the process of seducing the latest model he'd chosen from the list of contenders for signature model. "Damn it. I told her to hold my calls."

He pushed the girl away and snatched up the receiver. "What? I said no calls." He listened for a second and sank abruptly into his desk chair. "What is he talking about? Have you asked my wife?" Listened again. "Wait a minute, then put him through."

"Get out." He snarled at the model.

Tears filled her eyes and she stood still, "What did I do?"

"Just get out. Now." He buttoned his silk shirt and straightened his tie.

The girl pulled her skirt down, smoothed it and straightened her own blouse. Sniffling, she left his office.

The phone on his desk rang again and he snatched it up. "Who the hell are you? And what the hell are you talking about?"

The caller said, "Murder. And you better listen, Fontenburg. Maybe you should have a talk with your wife or a ton of trouble is coming down on you and your company."

"I haven't killed anybody. Say something that makes sense or I'm hanging up."

"The name Susan Kenyon, or Susie Penny, mean anything to you?"

Fontenburg felt the blood rush to his face. "Where are you? I think we better meet face-to-face. What's your name and I'll tell reception to let you come to my office."

The caller snorted. "Not hardly. I'm not getting anywhere near that cold-hearted bitch of a wife of yours. Dawgtown Bar, half an hour." Then dial tone came on the line as he hung up

Dave stormed back into Netria's office. He didn't notice the ashes he tracked across the carpet as he leaned over her desk.

Netria looked up from her cell phone, scowling, and laid it down beside another one on the side of her desk. "You again? I thought you were busy with the next lucky contender for our signature model opening."

"The opening we have because you finally found a reason to get rid of the best one we ever had?"

She jumped to her feet and faced him. "You mean the one who rebuffed you? But you weren't about to give up on? Heather Kenyon?"

"What's it to you? You have your boy toys."

"Only they don't threaten to bring down the company like your tom-catting around." She retorted.

He shook his fist in her face. "Neither did Heather. But you thought you saw your chance to get rid of her."

"I saw the chance to get rid of two threats to the company. You should thank me. How many models do you think would succumb to your non-existent charm if you weren't the big executive?"

"I don't recall that you were all that reticent." He taunted.

"When your playing around caught up with you, you were too squeamish to do what needed to be done. If you'd got rid of that little bitch when she blackmailed you we wouldn't be in this spot now."

"Or we'd be in prison." He shot back.

She continued as though he hadn't spoken. "So I had to take care of it over twenty-five years later."

His face blanched as he dropped suddenly into the chair in front of her desk. "You? You did kill her?"

"Don't be a bigger fool than you have to be. Of course I didn't do it myself."

"You mean - you hired somebody? Now who's the fool? They can lead the cops right to you. And me, too. The s.o.b. is expecting me to meet him in a few minutes."

They both jumped when the voice of Netria's secretary came through the telephone intercom.

"Mrs. Fontenburg?"

Netria pressed the button. "What is it, Leanna? I told you I didn't want to be disturbed."

"There's a policeman here, a detective. He wants to talk to you."

"Well, what does he want to talk to me about?"

There was silence on the line, then the assistant came back. "He says it's very important and he won't take much of your time."

"Very well. Five minutes. Send him in."

Dave had already slipped through the connecting door of their offices. She jabbed the end of her cigar into the ashtray her assistant had replaced on the desk without comment. Sergeant McAlester came through her outer office door.

He displayed his ID folder. "Detective Sergeant Jud McAlester, Mrs. Fontenburg. I appreciate you seeing me."

"How can I help you, Sergeant?" Netria did not ask him to sit, so he remained standing.

"You can help me by telling me who called you on Tuesday night, or rather very early Wednesday morning, at two a.m."

Netria's laugh sounded a little forced. "You can't be serious. I was sound asleep. If someone rang my phone, I didn't hear it."

McAlester took a folded paper from his pocket and laid it on the desk. "The call duration was almost twenty minutes. Did the person leave a voice mail message for you? Be advised, ma'am, we can subpoena your phone records. And your phone."

Netria's expression was a study in fury, indecision and fear. "Are the police accustomed to interfering in the business activities of a private citizen, Sergeant?"

"No, ma'am, unless it impinges on a murder investigation."

"Lady Veronica is hardly likely to be involved in a murder." The ice in her voice was a bit broken. Her eyes moved toward the phones on her desk and quickly back.

McAlester glanced at the carpet. He noted the ash and the footprints leading to a doorway. "Perhaps your husband answered the phone early this morning?"

"My husband does not answer my phone. He has his own."

"Then please check your call history and tell me who your early morning caller was. And what your conversation was about."

Her hands on the desk were clenched. "I certainly will not. The call concerned Lady Veronica business."

"You just said you didn't hear it ring." He pointed out.

"I checked it later." She snapped.

"Very well." He laid another sheet of paper on the desk. "This is a subpoena ordering you to surrender your mobile phone in order for us to examine its call log."

"This is an outrage. I'm calling my attorney." She almost screamed.

"By all means. If he doesn't understand, I'll be glad to explain what a subpoena is to him." He dropped into one of the chairs near her desk uninvited. "Mind if I sit while you consult with your attorney? Thank you."

If looks could kill, he would have died on the spot. She grabbed her phone and punched the intercom, "Leanna, call Silas Vail and tell him to get over here. Don't accept any excuses. Get him."

Half an hour later a nervous looking Silas Vail entered Netria's office. "What's this about, Mrs. Fontenburg?"

"Ask him." She replied, venom in her voice.

McAlester had risen to his feet, holding out his credentials. The lawyer examined them carefully. "What is it you want of my client, Sergeant?"

"A judge has signed the subpoena there on her desk instructing her to surrender her mobile phone to the police department for examination."

"To what purpose?"

"It's in the subpoena, counselor. We have reason to suspect that your client was in contact with a person or persons who kidnapped two people two nights ago, and that person or persons attempted to murder those two people."

"Why would my client be in contact with such people? She is a respected business owner."

"That is one of the questions we would like answered."

"Who is this person or persons? Have you asked my client if she knows them?"

"We do not have the name. We have a mobile phone they used, which was used to call your client's mobile phone. She claims the call was related to her business. We need the person's name to verify that. And the nature of her 'business' with that person."

"And if she chooses not to comply?"

McAlester took another paper from his inside jacket pocket. "Then she will be arrested. This is a warrant for her arrest if she makes that choice."

Vail visibly wilted. He spread his hands toward Netria. "I'm afraid you have no choice, Netria. Give him your phone unless you want to be arrested."

"Damn you! Do something! What good are you?" She jumped to her feet. "You're not getting my phone." She grabbed one of the phones on the desk, threw it on the floor, and started to raise her foot in its four inch wedge heel to stomp on it. But McAlester had edged closer to the desk and grabbed her arms, quickly snapping cuffs around her wrists.

He told Vail, "Perhaps you can explain to your client that she now has another charge against her. Attempting to destroy evidence." He told Vail.

While McAlester read her Miranda rights to his client Vail stood as though in shock.

"You'll pay for this, I'll have your badge."

"Doubtful." McAlester propelled her through the door.

She screamed at her assistant, "Find my husband. And you, Vail, better not let them keep me. You'll find it hard to practice law without a license."

Netria's assistant stood frozen and the attorney's face lost even more color.

Chapter Thirty-Four

After Dana reported that Jon was still doing well, Willa and Heather headed straight for the ladies restroom to freshen up and change clothes. Bret was in Jon's room. Gaby stayed in the waiting room long enough to give Dana the garments they had purchased for her. Dana declared that they could not have chosen anything more to her liking.

Gaby then filled her mother in on the excitement at Susan's apartment and Heather's discovery of the flash drives. Dana was a little alarmed when told of the fake car service driver, but reassured when Gaby said she'd had her gun with her.

"But I'm glad you didn't have to shoot anyone. We don't need any more police entanglement. "She sighed. "I do hope there's information on the flash drives that will bring this investigation to a conclusion."

"It was important enough for her to hide it. So it must mean something. Maybe something to do with - that business." Gaby replied.

"Yes." Dana leaned back and closed her eyes. "I'm still having trouble really believing all we've been told about Tod. Our whole lives a sham, from the beginning."

"Maybe we can put it behind us when Susan's killer is discovered and..." Gaby's voice trailed off.

"After the trial? We'll get through that, too. With each other's support, we will." Dana opened her eyes and squeezed Gaby's hand. "Now let's go get changed ourselves. Here's Willa and Heather."

When Gaby and Dana returned in their fresh clothing, Jud McAlester had arrived. He, Bret and Jon's doctor were deep in conversation.

"He should be fine to answer your questions. Just try and limit it to about fifteen minutes. He had very serious injuries and is still in early recovery."

McAlester nodded. "I understand. I'll keep it as brief as possible."

Jon looked toward the door as McAlester came into his room. He lay on his back and a brief expression of pain passed over his face as his broken arm moved a little. "Hello, Sergeant. They've told me about you."

"Mr. Blessing. Do you feel up to talking a little?" McAlester came to the side of the bed.

"Sure. I'd like to get my hands on the guys who beat up on me when you catch them."

McAlester smiled. "I think you'll have to stand in line. They are very unpopular with your family, too."

Jon started to nod, thought better of it. "Sit down, Detective."

McAlester pulled a chair closer to the bed. "Your sister has told us what happened up until you got separated. Can you tell me what you remember about the night she came to your house?"

"Okay. I was surprised, to put it mildly, when I opened the door and there she stood. So much like Heather, only more mature. I just stood there, stupefied. I'd looked for her so long, and here she was, on my doorstep. She said something like, 'Are you my brother?' I stammered out something. Maybe 'I think so.' And finally invited her in." He smiled. "It was like Christmas when you're a kid, how you've wished for and wanted something so long and then on Christmas morning, there it is."

"You were both very happy to find each other?"

"Oh, yeah. And we'd barely scratched the surface of getting acquainted. I started to call Bret, Mr. Kenyon, to see if they were still up so I could take Willa to meet Heather. And that thug was in the kitchen." Jon's expression darkened and his free hand clenched.

"I know it's difficult. But what happened then?" McAlester had his phone out, taking notes.

"He let the other guy in and I asked what they wanted, then he hit me with the gun in his hand. I was dazed, but I heard the phone ring. My answer machine picked up and Heather said she'd be at my house in a few minutes. It scared me even more to think she'd walk in on what was happening. The guy who hit me ordered Willa to help me into her car and the other guy to drive my truck. I leave the keys in it."

He still had several telemetry leads attached to his body. The heart rate monitor ratcheted up and McAlester glanced at it. "Relax a minute. The nurse will come and throw me out."

Jon made an effort to relax against the pillows. After a minute the monitor settled down again. "We left the house and at least I knew they wouldn't get Heather, but I was still scared for Willa. Afraid they were going to kill us, but I didn't know why."

"You were still semi-conscious?" McAlester asked.

"Yes. But I know the roads in that part of the county like the back of my hand. I tried to memorize the turns they made. When we got to the Stanhope place I knew where we were. Actually only about three miles from the Kenyon place." He reached for the plastic glass of water on his bedside table, took a sip.

"They took us into the enclosed shed in back that the Stanhopes use as a garage. There's a junk room in the back. They tied us back to back to a pole in the middle of it. We managed to get loose and broke through the door to the main part of the building. My truck and Willa's car were there but no keys. I was going to hot-wire my truck when we saw lights through the glass in the smaller door beside the big sliding door. We ran out. As their car came around the corner of the house, the headlights hit us and I pushed Willa, told her to run and hide, I'd catch up. I ran in a different direction, but tripped at a ditch and my head hit a rock. That's all I remember until I came to in a different place."

McAlester looked up. "Tell me about that. Did you recognize where you were?"

"No idea. It seemed to be a basement of a house. My hands and feet were tied to a chair. Cold water had been thrown in my face and was dripping down my shirt. One guy sat on a sofa. The bigger guy was in front of me with a bucket in his hands. 'Welcome back, Now answer some questions or you'll get worse than cold water in the face. Where is it?' I asked him where was what and he slapped me. It went on for a while, I don't know how long." Jon rubbed his face and ear as though remembering the pain.

McAlester waited a minute, then asked, "Did he ever say what 'it' was?"

"No. Just kept hitting me and saying things like, 'Didn't your loving Mama give you something to keep for her?' And I kept telling him she hadn't. By the time he stopped, I was going in and out of consciousness. I went out again as he was leaving the room. Then I came to for a little when he and the other guy came back. They were arguing."

"About what?"

"The other guy was saying he didn't sign up for murder. Kidnapping was bad enough, but murder would get you the death penalty. The big guy said, 'So we don't get caught. Help me get him in the truck.' Then he walked over and just hit me in the jaw with his fist and that is the last I remember until I woke up in ICU." He waved his hand, palm up. "Now can you tell me what you know about what happened to me? Bret said one of the men is in custody?"

"Yes. He turned himself in. He's not talking a lot. He wants to work a deal with the DA before he'll say more."

"A deal! Which one is it?"

"Says he's not the one who beat up on you or put you in your truck and rolled it. But he won't give us the other one. Or where they kept you when they 'questioned' you." McAlester put quote marks around the word questioned. "Can you remember anything, any little detail, about the place?"

Jon closed his eyes. "I figured it was a basement because there was ductwork along the ceiling. An old dingy sofa was along one wall. A couple of windows with inside shutters half-way up, brown, I think. Two doors, one looked like an outside door. The other led to another part of the basement, I just got a glimpse. It looked more furnished, dark green carpet, the corner of a table."

"Any other furniture besides the old sofa in the room where you were?"

"No-o-o. Not furniture."

McAlester's gaze sharpened. "But what?"

"As I said, the shutters went partway up on the windows. The glass part I could see reflected something on the wall behind me."

"Okay."

"It was blue at the top, dark green below, oval-shaped. A figure stood beside something, some kind of structure, I think, open but had a roof. His elbow stuck out, he seemed to hold something to his mouth."

"You didn't recognize it?"

"No-o-o, and the reflection was kind of blurry."

"Okay. When they left the room, they went through the inside door?"

"Yes. But they just opened it wide enough to get through and I was bleary..." His voice trailed away.

McAlester said softly, "You remembered something else?"

"I think - think I heard another voice."

"Sex?"

"Male. Or else a woman with a masculine-sounding voice."

"Any words?"

"No, well, a swear word or two. 'G-D, shut...' That's all."

"Any sense of recognition of the voice?"

Jon began to shake his head, must have remembered it hurt, said, "No."

McAlester stood to his feet. "I'll let you rest before they drag me out of here. If you remember anything else–"

"Will sure let you know. Oh, were there any fingerprints in or on my truck?"

"No. Either gloves or wiped clean." McAlester opened the door, said, "Thank you. Hope you heal quickly."

He felt the gaze of five pairs of eyes land on him as he entered the waiting room again. Bret spoke first, "Was he able to give you any information that would help find this other guy?"

"Not immediately." McAlester drew a chair near the group and sat down. "Apparently two men interrogated him in the basement of a house before they tried to kill him by rolling his truck with him inside."

"But he didn't know where?"

"No. Since the assault happened in Sweetwater County, I expect Sheriff Glass and his detective will be wanting to talk to Jon now that he's out of danger."

"Well, they can wait a few hours. My patient has to rest." The doctor had approached without their notice. "He seems to have weathered your questioning, Sergeant, but he's very tired. I told the nurse I don't want him disturbed for at least a couple of hours."

"Yes, Doctor." Bret said. "We'll go have a leisurely lunch. You have my numbers, if you need us for anything."

The doctor nodded and left the waiting room.

Chapter Thirty-Five

The Kenyon entourage started to follow, but McAlester held up a hand to stop them. "Let's go to the cafeteria and I'll fill all of you in on something that happened earlier."

When they had gathered around a table, he stated, "I arrested Netria Fontenburg and she is being questioned at headquarters."

Shock held the entire group quiet for a few seconds. Then several spoke at once.

"How in God's name is she involved in all this?" Bret burst out.

"Netria? How - what?" Heather asked.

"Who is Netria what? Fontenburg?" Willa looked puzzled.

Heather explained. "One of my former employers."

"A call to her mobile phone number was on the disposable phone in the possession of the suspect who turned himself in." McAlester explained. "She refused to give up her phone or explain the call. I had anticipated that reaction and also obtained an arrest warrant, should she refuse."

"Has she said anything?" Bret asked.

"Not so far. And her husband is in the wind. We have an APB out on him as a person of interest." He stood. "Well. On that note, I'll leave you to go have your lunch. I've just had a text from Sheriff Glass that he and his Chief Deputy Corbett will be here this afternoon."

"Thanks, Sergeant. Let us know if you find out anything else." Bret also stood and everyone followed suit. "We'll be at Uptown Eats, if that's agreeable with everyone." He looked around as heads nodded agreement.

Two and a half hours later they had again gathered in the waiting room of the step-down ICU unit. They were barely settled when Sheriff Glass and Deputy Corbett arrived.

They shook hands with Bret and touched their hats to the ladies. "Say our boy is doing a lot better, Bret?" Glass asked.

"Yes, Cal. I'm sure he'll be happy to help you catch the guy who beat him any way he can."

"Bad business. He up to seeing us now?"

"Yes, the doctor said so after he'd had a couple hours rest and he has. I was about to go in to see him. I'll take you."

The two lawmen followed Bret, surprisingly light on their feet for their sizes.

Bret knocked softly and the three men entered Jon's room. "Jon, I think you met Sheriff Glass at Dana's and my wedding. This is Chuck Corbett, his Chief Deputy."

"Glad to see you, Sheriff. Deputy." Jon replied.

"And we're glad you're coming along well," Sheriff Glass replied.

Bret walked over and patted Jon's cast. "Jon, since your kidnapping and assault occurred in Sweetwater County, the case is under his jurisdiction. That's why he needs to question you about it."

"Sure," Jon said, but his eyes were fixed on the shoulder of the Sheriff's uniform. Then he looked at Deputy Corbett's shoulder patch.

Glass looked at his own shoulder, an uneasy look on his face. Glass might be a country sheriff, but he was far from stupid. "Something about my uniform patch, son?"

"Uh, maybe." Jon's glance toward Bret was also uneasy.

"Want to tell me what it is about the patch?" Glass asked.

"Uh, I saw something similar in the basement room where those men held me and one of them beat me."

Bret looked as puzzled as Deputy Corbett. They all waited for Jon's explanation.

"It was on the wall behind the chair I was tied to. Reflected in the upper part of the windows in front of me, the part not covered with shutters."

"A picture?" Glass prodded.

"I'm not sure. I don't think so. It was round, or oval, showed a figure beside some kind of structure, holding something to his mouth. Like the guy on your patches."

"Original Sweetwater County logo." Glass spoke softly. "We like it, have managed to be the last county organization to get the new one on our uniforms."

Bret walked over and examined the logo on the Sheriff's shoulder. "What is it?"

"A person with a dipper drinking water from the well of cold, sweet water the county's named for. The framework structure is over the well, had a windlass that drew the water up."

"Is there significance in Jon seeing that mural, seal, whatever, in that room?" Bret asked.

Glass and Corbett exchanged a long look. Turned back to Jon. "Maybe. But let's go over everything that happened right now."

Bret went to lean against the window sill and the Sheriff sat in the chair beside Jon's bed. Corbett stood at the foot of the bed.

After Jon had given the same account of his ordeal he had given McAlester, he lay back and waited to see if they would provide any information in return.

Sheriff Glass hoisted himself to his feet and said, "Thank you, Mr. Blessing. I know you'd like to know what we might suspect. But as of right now it would only be speculation. I need to talk to Detective McAlester to get his thoughts on how his case and ours, yours, might be connected."

"You mean my birth mother's murder?"

"They did ask you if she gave you anything. That would certainly indicate a connection. Hopefully we'll soon have some answers."

"Cal, you have a suspect in mind, don't you?" Bret demanded, as they returned to the waiting room.

"Just an idea, Bret. It could be all wet. We'll get to the bottom of this. First kidnapping we've had in Sweetwater County in years. I aim for it to be the last for as many more."

"All right. Thanks, Cal."

The Sheriff and his deputy left after again touching their hats to the women in the room.

"Bret, did Jon remember something that will help them catch his and Willa's attackers?" Dana took Bret's arm as he walked back to the group.

"I think so, honey. But I've no idea what it means."

"Tell us, Daddy." Heather hung on his other arm. "Was it something about the men?"

"I don't think so. It was something in the room they held him in that resembled the old county logo."

They all exchanged puzzled glances. "The old county logo?" Dana said. "Was it changed at some point?"

"Apparently so. The Sheriff's Department has not adopted the new one on their uniforms yet and Jon noticed it."

"Well, I hope it helps. Those awful men nearly made me lose my brother, again." The expression on Willa's face did not bode well for the men, if she encountered them.

Gaby had a thoughtful look on her face. "The day I was in Lily Springs and the man accosted and warned me, I saw that logo, twice."

Bret asked, "Did you tour the old courthouse, Gaby? It's on the wall in front of you as you go in the main entrance."

"I just peeked in. I wanted to see Mom's, and your, old school so I didn't take the courthouse tour."

"So where else did you see it?"

Gaby took a moment to answer. Dana repeated her question.

"Oh, sorry, Mom. It was when County Attorney Yates Orton gave me a lift to the Sheriff's lab. A slick printed copy of the person standing by a well was attached to the sun visor of his car."

"I guess he likes it."

"Uh huh." Gaby said in an absent voice, her expression still thoughtful.

"Is there something else about that day, Gaby?"

"Um. I don't know. Has Sheriff Glass mentioned the results of the lab test on the blood under my fingernails?"

"Not that I know of. Maybe we better ask him."

"Maybe they were backed up and the results aren't available yet." But Gaby didn't sound as if she believed it.

Bret pulled out his phone and went into the hallway. The waiting room now held a number of other visitors and the noise level had risen.

When he returned to the group his expression did not portend good news.

"What did Sheriff Glass say, Bret?" Dana asked.

"Let's go to the cafeteria so we can talk about it." He suggested.

When they had gotten coffee and were gathered around their usual corner table, Bret answered Dana's question. "He knew nothing about a test done on material from under Gaby's fingernails."

Consternation showed on everyone's face. "How can that be?" Willa asked, at the same time Gaby said, "Say what?"

"He's going to find out. He was fit to be tied. He and Corbett were about to head back to Lily Springs. I expect he'll get an answer within a couple of hours. Or know the reason why."

Bret turned toward Gaby. "You did say Yates Orton took you to the Sheriff's lab for the testing?"

"Yes. And I saw the county logo for the second time in his car." Gaby answered.

"I was in Jon's room when Glass questioned him. He and the Chief Deputy reacted a little oddly when Jon described it. I thought it was just because it was the old one, not the location. Now I wonder."

Gaby mused, as if thinking out loud. "Add that to the fact the Sheriff didn't know about the test on the blood under my nails. I think something is not too sweet in Sweetwater County."

"I think you might be right. And I'm beginning to wonder about Yates Orton."

"Bret! Honey, you can't be jealous of Yates. He's harmless." Dana exclaimed.

"Is he? Gaby, did Yates Orton just happen by when the man accosted you?"

"As far as I know. He came out of a shop just down from the old courthouse. A ladies clothing shop, I think."

Bret turned to Dana. "Did Yates have family? Mother still alive? Sister maybe?"

"As I recall, he was an only child." She said.

"I don't think his parents are still living. I seem to remember when he was appointed District Attorney it was said he was the last of a long-time county family."

"So, why would he be coming out of a ladies clothing shop?" Gaby asked.

"Aunt? Female friend? Bret, what are you thinking?"

"Last of the line, they said, honey. I don't know. Just exploring– " He broke off when Dana's expression changed. "What did you just remember?"

"He dated Susan a few times when we were freshmen. But she broke it off. Said he was not her type."

Willa's face paled. She whispered, "How old was she when you were freshmen, Dana?"

"She would have been fourteen, I was just a little younger." Dana replied, then gave Willa a startled look. "Oh, Lord, you're thinking - he might be..."

"Our 'sperm donor,' as Jon called whoever our biological father is. Could he?"

"I honestly don't know. My memory isn't clear enough on the months she was gone. But I guess, maybe it's possible."

They discussed the implications of Yates Orton being involved in their troubles for a while. Then Bret looked at Willa, "Maybe you'd better go up to Jon's room for a few minutes. He's had time to relax a little from the Sheriff's visit. He'll be wondering why someone hasn't come in to see him."

"I was thinking the same thing. But I'm not telling him anything about all this until we know more."

"I think that's best, too." Bret agreed.

"We'll wait around, then a couple more of us can see him, then we'll go to dinner."

When Willa had gone upstairs, Heather said, "Gaby, let's hit the gift shop before it closes and get him something. A manly bouquet of something and anything else that appeals."

Bret reached for his wallet to give her his credit card.

"Oh, no, you don't, Dad." Heather laughed and waved it away. "Buy your own manly flowers for him."

All four wound up examining the gift shop offerings for the cheer and comfort of patients. After making their choices and paying, they trooped back up to the waiting room. Bret and Heather took the gifts and flowers to Jon's room and Willa joined Gaby and Dana.

"How is he? Did the Sheriff's visit upset him?" Dana asked.

"No, it didn't seem to. He was somewhat puzzled at their reaction about the county logo he saw reflected in the window."

"Were you able to deflect him from it?"

"I think so. I couldn't think of anything else that would, so I told him about not hearing any results about the lab test on your fingernails." She told Gaby. "That puzzled him, too, of course."

Bret and Heather rejoined them in about forty-five minutes and they decided to return to the hotel and order room service again.

Chapter Thirty-Six

The server had just brought their dinner to the room and departed when Sergeant McAlester called from the lobby. Bret invited him to come on up to the suite.

"We'll be happy to share our dinner, Sergeant." Bret told him as he opened the door after McAlester's knock.

"Thanks, but I've just had a couple of Varsity hot dogs. I'll take a cup of coffee though."

When everyone was seated, food and drink blessed, McAlester looked around the group. "Some news that may shock you a little. David Fontenburg was apprehended at the airport, a one-way ticket to Brazil in his pocket. He insists he wasn't involved with whatever his wife was into. Tried to call the company lawyer, but he couldn't reach him."

"That sleaze is in it up to his neck," Bret exclaimed. "I'd bet on it."

"You could be right," McAlester agreed. "He left his last firm under a bit of a cloud. Mr. Kenyon, how long have you known your District Attorney, Yates Orton?"

Dana glanced at Bret, but he was staring at McAlester. "About all my life. Why?"

"Is he a friend or business acquaintance with the Fontenburgs?"

"The Fonten - ," Bret's expression grew more puzzled. "I had no idea they even knew each other. Do they?"

"We've reason to think they do. How often do you see Mr. Orton?"

"Seldom, actually. Our wedding was the first time I'd seen him since I attended a County Commission meeting on new zoning regulations several years ago. I've had no problems with the county in the eighteen years or so I've been back."

"So I suppose you've known District Attorney Orton a long time, too, Mrs. Kenyon?"

"Yes, I knew they were a prominent family in the county when we were all growing up. But he was a couple years ahead of me in high school. I never really knew him except as an upper class fellow Sweetwater High student."

Gaby's and Bret's eyes met, both raised eyebrows slightly.

McAlester did not miss the interaction. "Something else, Mr. Kenyon?"

"Oh, he's just a little peeved at a look he imagined Yates Orton gave me at the wedding." Dana's voice held a little irritation.

Gaby touched her mother's hand. "Mom, I saw the look in his eyes when he talked about you the day we were having coffee. I think he had a crush on you, without you knowing it maybe."

"Mrs. Kenyon, as I told you before about Mr. Pennington's possible early designs on you, there is no reflection on your character. I'm sorry, but it's possible there is also a connection from back then to the present involving Mr. Orton."

"Can you be a little more specific, McAlester? What kind of connection are you talking about?" Bret demanded.

McAlester looked around the group, apparently considering what or how much he could reveal. "Calls between the Fontenburgs and Mr. Orton. Some references to Tod Pennington, years ago and in the more recent past. Some with correlation to what was discovered in company records in Illinois."

"Have the police uncovered anything about the car service driver who ditched us?" Heather asked.

Just then McAlester's phone sounded a two-note chime to indicate receiving a text. He looked down and read it. "I'm sorry, I have to go. A new development. I'll keep you informed as much as I'm able."

After McAlester left they stacked the dishes on the room service cart and Bret pushed it into the corridor.

Coming from the bedroom with her purse Gaby announced, "Mom, I'm going to the farm to get more clothes. It's early, I should be back by bedtime."

"May I go, too? My suitcase is still in my car." Willa snapped her fingers. "Oh, and the car is still in impound."

Bret pulled out his phone and began paging through his contacts. "I'll call the Sheriff and see if he can get the car released so you can get your suitcase." He dialed the number and while waiting for the ring on the other end, pulled his keys out and said, "You can drive the Cadillac. I'd prefer you didn't use the car service again until we hear something from McAlester."

"Thanks. I wasn't too keen on it myself." Gaby grinned.

But Bret didn't get an answer when he rang the Sheriff's cell phone. So he looked up the main Sheriff's Department number. Deputy Hart Wilson answered. "Sheriff Glass and Deputy Corbett are at Raymond Evans's home. Our lab tech that you met at your place. Do you know what that's about, Mr. Kenyon?"

"Not sure, Hart. I expect he'll fill you in. I'm calling about the car belonging to Jon Blessing's sister. Her luggage is in it and she'd like to get it from impound. Is that possible?"

"Maybe. They'll be closing in half an hour. Is she still here in Sweetwater County?"

"No, we're in Atlanta, but she and Gaby, my - my wife's daughter are driving out to the farm. They can be in Lily Springs in about an hour and a half."

"Okay. I'll meet them there and get it released. We're finished with it." Hart gave directions to the impound lot a couple of miles from the Sheriff's office. "Here's my cell number if they have trouble finding the place."

"Appreciate this, Hart."

"No problem." Hart said and ended the call.

"Bret, I've decided to go with the girls to the farm." Dana's purse was on her shoulder and she, Gaby and Willa were ready to leave.

"Sure, honey. Take care, all of you."

Willa said, "Be sure and let us know, if, God forbid, there's any change in Jon's condition while we're gone."

"Of course, but I'm sure he'll be fine."

"Wanna drive, Mom?" Gaby asked as the valet brought the silver Lexus around to the hotel entrance.

"No, you drive, honey. I know you'd rather." Dana smiled.

The forty minute drive to Sweetwater County was uneventful, Interstate traffic not too heavy. When they reached Lily Springs the GPS on the Lexus took them to the address Deputy Hart had given Bret. It was a run-down looking business with a rickety looking board fence around the lot beside it.

"Can this be it?" Dana wondered. "Surely, the county can afford a better place to store the cars they impound."

"One would think." Gaby echoed.

"Maybe we should wait until the Deputy gets here before we get out." Willa's voice sounded a little nervous.

"I'll peek through the window. If I can see anything through the dirt." Suiting action to word Gaby opened her door.

As she stepped out of the car a plain dark sedan drove up and parked beside the Lexus. Deputy Wilson got out and spoke as he came around his vehicle. "Brought my personal car since I'm off-duty. Come on, we'll see if we can roust anybody. Should be a watchman."

Wilson went to a gate in the fence and unlocked the padlock holding it closed. He stood back to let them precede him through the opening. Dana turned back and started to say, "Deputy, are you sure this..." Her words trailed off as she found herself staring at the business end of a revolver.

Gaby had turned, too, and saw the gun. "What the hell? Are you mad, Deputy Wilson?'

"No, and I really wish Bret Kenyon hadn't called when DA Orton was in the squad room talking to me. I didn't want anything to do with any violence. I told him so."

Gaby sneered. "You just wanted the money."

"My old man was sick a long time. Left a mountain of medical bills there was no way I could get out from under on a deputy's salary."

"So Orton is somewhere building an alibi and you're left holding the bag." Gaby pointed a finger at Wilson. "Bret knows we're here. With you."

"Oh, you won't be found here. The real impound yard is a mile down another road at the last crossroad. The number is the same as this place, only transposed. I waited, but you people never showed."

Dana stared at the deputy. "You're a fool. You will be caught. Yates Orton always found a way to blame others for things he did in high school."

Gaby and Willa exchanged a quick look. Gaby seized the opportunity to nod slightly toward the deputy while he was focused on Dana. "Talk." She mouthed.

Willa jumped in with the first thing she could think of to say, "He's already under suspicion. You both have somebody watching you now."

Deputy Hart's head moved slightly to try and look behind him. He must have glimpsed Gaby raising her purse and started to move his gun to point at her. But she fired through the purse and her bullet was faster. It struck him under the right shoulder blade and his weapon dropped from nerveless fingers, firing into the ground. Gaby moved quickly to kick it away.

Chapter Thiry-Seven

Five minutes after Gaby shot Wilson several Sheriff's Department cars and a couple of unmarked vehicles skidded to a stop and armed men poured from them. The road in front of the run-down business was filled with blue lights and sirens. A wailing ambulance brought up the rear.

Atlanta PD Detective Sergeant Jud McAlester leapt from one of the unmarked cars and managed to reach Gaby first. "Are you all right, Gaby?" He demanded, grabbing both her arms, pulling her closer.

Willa whispered to Dana and Heather, "Guess we're chopped liver, huh?"

Dana smiled a little shakily and nodded.

Gaby looked into McAlester's eyes. She had to swallow before she could reply, "I'm fine, Sergeant. I guess you better step back though, I think the Sweetwater police will be wanting my weapon."

"Um, yes, ma'am. I do have to ask for you to hand it over." Chief Deputy Corbett reached for her purse. Gaby shrugged it from her shoulder.

"I guess you have to keep the purse, too, don't you?"

"Afraid so. We'll get it back to you as soon possible after Evans finishes with it."

McAlester intervened. "Don't mean to interfere, Deputy, but can't she keep her ID? She won't be able to drive without it."

"Tell you what. You'll be needing to go to the Department anyway to go over what happened. After we verify identity and that it is your purse, I think the Sheriff will let you keep your ID."

Sheriff Glass stood in front of his wounded deputy, face hard, ignoring the man's bleeding shoulder. "Wilson, you're under arrest. If there's proof you killed or assaulted anyone, I'll do my damn best to make sure you get the maximum penalty." He herded Wilson toward the ambulance as paramedics approached.

The sheriff motioned for Corbett to ride in the ambulance with the prisoner. "Don't let this bastard out of your sight."

"Yes, sir."

The sheriff turned to the four women. "Do any of you need these emergency medics to look you over?"

"No, thank you, Sheriff Glass. He didn't have a chance to hurt us, thanks to Gaby." Dana answered.

"If you're sure, then. If one of you feels up to driving, you can follow me to the station. We'll get your statements and you can call your husband or he'll have my - er, head."

"We'll follow, Sheriff. Well, Mom, I guess you'll have to drive. Is that okay?"

Dana nodded. "Yes. I'll drive."

They got into the Lexus and the official cars cleared a way for Dana to pull into the county road and drive away. When they reached the sheriff's station, he was standing in front and waved for her to park beside his official space. They followed him into the station.

Before Dana could call Bret, he called her. She answered and told him an abbreviated version of events. Then she asked Sheriff Glass to talk to him. Glass assured Bret they were all fine and would be heading back to Atlanta as soon as their statements were taken.

Two hours later they were back on the road to the city, after a hurried stop at home to grab a few clothes.

Gaby was again driving, the Sheriff having returned her driver's license and a couple other essential pieces of identification. He promised to bring her purse to her the next day.

"I'm not really sure what clothing I threw in the suitcase for us." Dana said after a few miles. "Everything will probably clash."

"Dad - Bret won't care." Gaby replied.

Willa was in the back seat, on the driver's side and caught Gaby's eye in the rear view mirror. "May I ask a personal question? If you don't want to answer, it's all right."

"Sure, fire away." Gaby gave a rueful smile, "So to speak."

"You've seemed, well, you seemed to have a different attitude toward Bret today. Like you almost call him 'Dad' instead of 'Bret.'"

Gaby looked toward her Mother. "Mom?"

Dana turned slightly to the side to speak to Willa. "We finally told Gaby the truth. It was way past time, but the revelations about her father, as she thought, made it imperative. Bret is her biological father. I was pregnant when I married Tod Pennington. He knew, and he knew who the father was. And he was an absolute low-life, we've discovered."

"I'm sorry about that." Willa said softly. "But I'm glad you know who your father is. I hope Jon and I will be glad when we know who is our 'sperm donor.'"

"Could you live with not knowing?" Dana asked.

"I'm not sure about Jon. I think I could, now that I've found my brother."

They were silent much of the rest of the trip, trying to talk only about inconsequential topics.

Bret and Heather met them in the lobby of the hotel. Predictably Bret berated himself, "Thank God, none of you were hurt. I should have gone."

"We're all okay. And apparently there's been a big breakthrough on the case, but we don't know the details. Maybe Sheriff Glass and Sergeant McAlester can fill us in tomorrow."

"Is Jon all right? When did you see him last?" Willa asked. "Is it too late to call him?"

"He insisted you call as soon as all of you got back. He's been moved to a private room and there's an officer outside his door. Just a precaution, he told us."

Willa immediately looked alarmed and grabbed her phone from her tote bag. Gaby touched her arm. "Just a second, Willa." She looked at Bret and Heather. "Does he know anything about what happened to us?"

Bret shook his head as Heather answered. "Oh, no. We didn't want to alarm him. He might have had a setback in his recovery."

"So, get calm, Willa. Take some deep breaths. We had an uneventful trip to get some of our things at the farm. We'll fill him in later."

"Right. Of course. I can't let him hear something to upset him in my voice." After she had talked to Jon and knew he really was okay, she told him to get some rest, she'd see him the next morning.

They ordered room service breakfast next morning and just as they finished up, Sheriff Glass called Bret. He asked if they would stay put for half an hour or so, that he and Sergeant McAlester would be there soon.

When the two lawmen arrived they accepted cups of coffee and everyone found seats in the living room of the suite.

Bret asked, "All right, Cal. Tell us what you've uncovered. I'm sorry one of your deputies turned out to be involved."

"Yeah, me, too. Especially who he is. It was a bad situation with Isaiah Wilson. Developed bone cancer and lingered longer than anybody expected. Left Hart with a mountain of medical bills."

"So how did Hart get mixed up in everything?"

"Who all was involved? Ever since—"Dana couldn't bring herself to finish the question.

"I'm afraid so, Mrs. Kenyon." The Sheriff said. "The man who kidnapped Ms. Younger and Mr. Blessing and turned himself in to the highway patrol decided he'd better talk or he might be blamed for everything.

"He didn't know everything from the beginning though." Glass indicated Bret. "The beginning was some time before you became entrapped by your first wife, Susan Kent. As you know, she was, had been, involved in the paid female escort business, prostitution, since her teen years. Free lance at first, but someone who was a local handler in the business for Lily Springs, Sweetwater County and environs, couldn't allow a free lancer to cut into his business. So he forced her into his stable."

"It was Yates Orton, wasn't it?" Dana asked. Gaby took her hand and squeezed it.

Glass nodded.

"He wasn't a very nice person in school. But I never thought..." Dana's voice trailed away.

"He was actually into several underhanded activities while still in school, we've discovered. Classmates are willing to talk now."

"He and Susan?"

"And Tod Pennington. Tod was next in line in the escort business, Constant Services, above Yates Orton. He came out to evaluate Susan when Orton co-opted her into his local stable of girls. She fell in love with Orton and when she became pregnant she knew he was the father."

Glass waited for all his hearers to absorb what he had just said, before continuing. "She told him so he knew he was the father. She was actually glad. Though she knew he would never marry her for fear her background would someday come out. He couldn't take a chance on disgracing his family name, never mind what he was doing. But she wanted to have his baby.

"Orton tried to force her to have an abortion, but she refused. She had saved a small nest egg and persuaded her mother to send her to her out-of-state aunt's to have the baby. Or as it turned out, babies. Twins."

Willa and Gaby gasped. Dana had a dazed look on her face as she looked from Gaby to Willa.

Glass continued speaking when their attention returned to him. "She returned to Georgia, finished school and she was happy being near him again. Then Orton sent her to Atlanta and Tod Pennington took her over. Through the company, Tod met Dave Fontenburg and Netria Jones, another girl in the business."

Gaby looked surprised. "She isn't from India?"

"She was born in Indiaville, Alabama. She shortened the name and pretended she was from India when she ran away to Atlanta from an abusive home situation. We found the Family Services records."

Gaby looked as though she was doing some re-thinking.

"She was smart, though. She could have been a first-rate chemist, given the opportunity. She developed the early formulas for Lady Veronica cosmetics. When she revealed what she'd developed to Fortenburg and Tod Pennington, they decided to branch out into a legitimate business."

"But leopards can't change their spots, can they?" Dana said, softly.

"No, they can't. Fontenburg himself had fallen hard for Susan when she came to Atlanta and she became pregnant again."

Heather drew a deep breath. "So Fontenburg knew he was my biological father? And colluded with Susan to convince Dad that he was responsible."

"You may or may not be relieved to learn that he did not know he was your biological parent."

Relief and confusion mixed on her face. "Why not?"

"Who knew all this? Was it Yates Orton?" Bret asked, puzzlement in his voice.

"How do you know all that?" Willa frowned.

Comprehension dawned on Gaby's face. "The flash drives."

Glass nodded. "Susan had had any illusions knocked out of her, so she used her brain to try to cover herself. She kept secret records for years."

"So did she say on the drive that Fontenburg didn't know he had impregnated her?" Heather persisted.

Glass sighed. "By then the cosmetics business was taking off and Susan wanted a piece of the action. She knew Fontenburg wanted an heir and Netria couldn't give him one due to a botched abortion. And that one day when she lost her looks she'd be a liability to them."

"Blackmail." Gaby said.

"Yes. She went to Netria Fontenburg and made her demands. Or else she'd blow the whistle on everyone. But Netria wasn't about to give up any part of what got her out of prostitution. So Susan had to tell her about her secret records to save her life. It was a stalemate. Netria wanted Susan to get an abortion but again she refused, afraid she would be injured, too. Maybe deliberately."

Bret said, "So she tricked me into marriage, and then left when Heather was a few months old."

"Netria wanted her out of town. She sent her to Las Vegas, another stable. And apparently chose to forget about the child Susan bore."

"Damn lucky I sent her to boarding school in South Carolina, then. And that's where she first got noticed as a model."

Heather gave him a tight smile and nodded. "But I don't understand why they later chose me as their signature model."

Glass said, "That was Dave Fontenburg's doing. He thought he'd found his Susan again. His wife wasn't about to tell him you were his daughter. So she went along with it, until she could find a way to get rid of you."

"And recently Susan returned, again with blackmail in mind, but Netria wasn't taking any chances this time." Willa said.

"Exactly. She was sure they could find Susan's evidence. Only they couldn't and you ladies did."

Chapter Thirty-Eight

Bret and Perry Mitchell put legal paperwork in motion for Gaby's adoption before she finally got to Nashville for her internship interview with the white shoe law firm. Bret and Dana flew back to the Grand Canyon and enjoyed a three week delayed honeymoon.

Jon and Willa, along with Willa's son, met them at the airport on their return. "So you two are definitely moving to Georgia?" Bret asked Willa after they were In the helicopter on their way to Mill Creek Farm.

"Oh, yes. We're looking for a place for Billy and me. We can't thank you enough for letting us all stay in your house while you were gone and Jon's house being repaired. He has so loved helping care for the horses."

Billy looked up from the phone in his hand and his face lit up. "They're cool. Some day I want a horse of my own."

He bent his head to his phone again. "Cool as that phone?" Bret teased him.

"Aunt Heather bought it for me. I can play all kinds of cool games on it."

Bret tousled his hair. "I'm sure she loved getting it for you. She's tickled to have a nephew.

"We've been thinking about your housing situation, Willa. Since the security team is staying in the little apartment above the tack room, and Jon's house is a little small for three people, Dana—well, I'll let her tell you about it."

"I have that farmhouse just up the road that's going to be empty most of the time. I'd like to hire you, Willa, and Billy as caretakers for it."

"But - what about Gaby? Won't she want her privacy when she's there?"

"Gaby will be home very little for the next at least eighteen months. And she says she wants to stay with us when she is. That way when she and Heather are both home they'll be closer."

Willa swiped the corner of her eyes. "And we'd still be close to Jon. How could we ever repay you both for all you've done?"

"None needed. You two were almost–" Bret broke off and caught Jon's eye in the mirror above the windshield, nodded toward Billy.

"He knows all about what happened. Sis believes in full disclosure."

"Yes." Willa replied, directing a loving smile at her brother.

Bret continued what he had meant to say. "You two almost lost your lives because of mistakes in my past. It's I, we, who owe you."

"Indeed." Dana nodded vigorously.

Changing the subject, Bret asked Jon, "Any word from Glass? Or McAlester?"

Jon shook his head. "The second man is still out there. Or maybe he decided to cut out for parts unknown."

"With help from some of the dirty higher-ups in their organization, no doubt. I'm keeping security on us all until he's found."

"Won't it be difficult for them when Gaby starts her last year of law school?"

Bret sighed. "No more so than keeping up with Heather on her modeling assignments. Her agency is keeping her busy. She won't hear of slowing down. Says in her profession she has to 'make hay while the sun shines.'"

The chopper set down on the pad at the farmhouse and they all got out, ducking heads until they were out from under the rotors.

The senior security guard met them. "A word, Mr. Kenyon?"

"I've got your luggage, Bret." Jon called.

Bret waved the others to go on and walked with the security man to the gazebo in the side yard. "Anything wrong, Sol?"

"No. But this is almost the first of June. One of your employees mentioned that you always throw a big Fourth of July party. Invite a lot of people."

"I have in the last few years, yes."

"Are you going to do it this year? If so, how many people would you expect?"

Bret leaned against the wood lattice of the gazebo wall. "I've been thinking about that. In the past between two and three hundred people have shown up. My daughters will be here, too. Are you thinking security would be a problem?"

"With that many people? Oh, yeah."

"I'll talk to the Sheriff and Atlanta PD. For my family's safety, I might have to cancel the event this year."

Sol's eyes showed relief. "Might be wise. If you have it, I'd definitely advise beefing up security. Even with the guards watching your daughters added to the crew here."

"I'll let you know what I decide in a day or two, Sol."

The man sketched a salute and started to walk away. Bret made a motion to stop him and said, "Hold up. I forgot to tell you something. Ms. Younger and her son will be moving to my wife's farmhouse up the road. Since everyone won't be in one place now, add more men, if necessary."

"Will do, Mr. Kenyon. Are they going up there this evening?"

"No. I'll ask them to stay here tonight and move tomorrow."

"Right."

Chapter Thirty-Nine

Next morning Bret and Dana wandered into the kitchen in search of coffee. Willa reached for the insulated coffee carafe and filled the two cups waiting for them on the table. "Good morning, Scrambled eggs and toast? Coffee cake?"

"Coffee's good for now, thanks, Willa. You don't need to wait on us, you're not our housekeeper."

"Huh. For two people who've done so much for us, yes, I do." She replied. "And it's good to have you back, but I'm glad you had that lovely honeymoon, finally."

Dana touched her husband's hand. "It was lovely. But we're happy to be back home, too."

Bret picked up the remote and turned on the television tucked into the corner of the counter. "Billy sleeping in?"

"Hardly. As long as there are horses to feed, brush, walk, and ride."

Bret smiled. Just then a 'breaking news' banner flashed across the screen and they heard the voice of the anchor for metro news. "WANZ Atlanta has just learned of the arrest by the GBI of Sweetwater County Commission Chairman Rolf Manchester early this morning at his home. An anonymous source has reported the arrest is related to this past spring's revelations of sex trafficking in that county with tentacles into several states. The source also told WANZ that Mr. Manchester has asked to be placed in a secure facility. More details will be forthcoming as we learn them."

Consternation showed on the three faces around the table. Bret recovered first and snatched his cell phone from his shirt pocket. He hit a speed dial number and waited for an answer. They all heard the deep voice of Sheriff Cal Glass. "Figured you'd be calling when the news broke, Bret."

"Manchester? He was part of it?"

"Seems so. Not been released yet, but Yates Orton is dead."

"Dead? How?"

"Hung himself in his cell, supposedly."

"Was it suicide?"

"Unlikely. I can't give you any details, since the investigation is active. You still got your security at the farm, right?"

"You think there are even others locally?"

"Maybe. Or just the imported one we still haven't caught yet."

Willa's cup rattled a little as she set it in the saucer. "The one who beat Jon."

As soon as Bret ended the call, a thoughtful look on his face, his phone rang again. He looked at the display and quickly answered. "Heather! Baby, are you all right?"

"I'm fine, Daddy. How did you know?"

"Know what? Has something happened?"

"A prop fell during my shoot this morning. It grazed my temple and cheek, but I'm okay. Really. My bodyguard is insisting that I come home."

"Her face!" Dana breathed and put her hand over Bret's clenched fist pressing hard on the table.

"You better believe you're coming home. Let me talk to him, honey." He held the phone against his chest, "Willa, get Jon to the house immediately, please."

Speaking into the phone again, he asked. "Marvin, does Heather need medical care?"

He listened a minute. "Okay. Do not take her to the Polk airport. There's a big farm about five miles out of Rome, Pine Knot Farm, a friend owns it. He has a helo pad. I'll call him and have Jon meet you there. Hold on a minute, let me fill him in."

"The helicopter is ready to fly, right, Jon?"

"Always, Bret. Where do you–"

Bret interrupted him. "It's Heather. She's in Rome on a shoot and was injured slightly in an accident. If it was. We need to pick her up at Pine Knot Farm."

Jon 's face mirrored the fear on the other three. "Is she okay?"

"They say so. I won't be satisfied until I see her myself."

"She has three security guards. What about them?"

"We'll bring two back with us. The other can drive here."

With his hand on the door handle, Jon said, "We can be in the air in five minutes. Come on."

Bret stood, leaned over and kissed Dana. He was through the door right behind Jon as he spoke into his phone again to the bodyguard.

Two hours later the helicopter touched down on the helicopter pad at the Mill Creek Farm. Dana, Willa and Billy waited anxiously on the patio as the five people on board stepped off the chopper and hurried toward them. Billy ran to Heather and threw his arms around her. "Aunt Heather, you're okay, aren't you?" He touched the gauze taped to her cheek.

"Yes, honey. I am okay. It's sweet of you to worry about me."

Dana and Willa reached her and hugged her. "A doctor did treat you, right? Is it really just a scratch?" Willa demanded.

"Really, Willa. It'll be fine."

Just as they all started inside they heard engine noises. As the sounds got louder, they saw two vehicles on the long driveway approaching the house. First was Gaby's truck, but as it reached the turnaround everyone saw that Gaby was not the driver.

Dana jumped from the patio to the walkway around the house and dashed toward the front. She whirled around the corner as the truck and the dark green SUV behind it stopped at the wide front steps. She was almost at the driver's side door of the truck when she heard her daughter's voice. "Mom! Mom! Don't panic, here I am."

Dana stopped so suddenly she would have fallen, but the driver of the truck flung his door open and was beside her in time to catch her. He walked her to her daughter as Gaby ran to meet her. They embraced, then Dana held her away, looking her up and down. "Why is Trip driving your truck? And why did you come home?"

Gaby made a face. "They said I'd be safer in the SUV. But I wasn't about to leave my baby behind."

The rest of the family had arrived and Heather's bandage immediately caught Gaby's attention. She grabbed her. "Heather! Are you all right?"

"It's nothing. Tiny accident. Why did they bring you home?"

Gaby's three security guards and Marvin, who had followed the group to the front, automatically formed a perimeter around their charges. Their heads turned from side to side, their gaze roaming the area all around.

Bret hugged Gaby then turned to Marvin. "Is anyone around back?"

"Sol and Mike. Sol told me to stay with Heather."

"Okay. Good." He raised his voice slightly. "Everybody. Let's go inside and get everybody on the same page."

He looked at Marvin again. "Heather's other security should arrive within the hour. Trip and the others can cover the front. You help Sol cover the rear. Tell him I said to spread you all out however he thinks best."

"Will do." Marvin hurried back around the house.

Everyone gathered in the living room, but Dana caught Bret's eye before he spoke. He asked, "What is it, honey?"

"It'll be time for lunch soon. We have plenty of food for everyone in the freezer, but it would take a while to prepare it. Suggestions?"

Bret snapped his fingers. "Forgot. We made a stop at Barb's Beans n Things. Couple of large coolers of food in the chopper, we cleaned her out. She closed for the day."

"Pretty smart, aren't you, Mr. Kenyon?"

Everyone laughed, which relieved some tension. Jon spoke up. "Sol and I set them in the kitchen."

"Thanks, Jon. So let's see what's happened with everyone. We know about Heather's accident, and will fill you in, Gaby. But I need to know why Trip thought you should leave Nashville."

"Actually, I knew about the prop falling on Heather's photo shoot. I saw a Tweet from one of her fans. One of the photo assistants then tweeted that she was only scratched. But Marvin got a look at the support holding it up. He texted

Trip he thought it might have been tampered with and Dad and Jon were en route in the chopper to bring her home."

Dana cast an irritated glance toward Bret. "You didn't tell us about the tampering."

"Sweetheart, he wasn't sure. We decided to err on the side of caution. I didn't want to worry you any more than you were."

"We'll talk about that later. But, Gaby, did something happen in Nashville?"

"No, Mom. Well, no accident or anything." She shot a rueful grin at Heather. "I just got fired."

Consternation erupted from everyone at once.

"Fired?"

"What?"

"You're not serious?"

"'fraid so, Mom. The two senior partners called me in late yesterday and told me to clear out my desk. Which didn't take long since I'd only been there three weeks or so."

Bret leaned forward. "Did they give you a reason?"

"Actually they didn't have to, but they did, kind of. Of course, if I'd been a regular employee and not just an intern, it wouldn't hold up."

Heather remarked, "Sounds familiar."

"Go on, Gaby." Bret urged, as twin frown lines bisected his forehead.

"They said it had come to their attention that bodyguards followed me around. That they couldn't allow their firm and its employees to be put in any kind of danger and I should clear the hell out. Oops, sorry, Willa, forgot about Billy. Well, they didn't actually say that, but it's what they meant."

"They didn't ask you why you had bodyguards at all?"

"Nope. When I tried to get more information, one of them sent for security and told them to escort me from the premises. Which they did."

When several others began to ask more questions, Bret held up a hand. He punched a button on his phone and when the call was answered, said, "Trip, will you please come inside to the living room for a moment?"

205

When the tall, blond bodyguard entered he wore a sober expression. Bret stood up and said he had a few questions.

Trip said, "What do you want to know, sir?"

"Was there any particular reason you felt you should bring Ms. Pennington back here after her firm let her go?"

"Nothing I can put a finger on for sure, Mr. Kenyon. But when I escorted Gaby - Ms. Pennington into the office this morning a man I knew to be a senior partner was standing at the reception desk. The look he gave her, and then me, I can only describe as hostile. I was hesitant to leave, but I walked as far as the elevator bank. I stood in front of one maybe ten minutes when two men in building security uniforms stepped off another one and entered the law firm. A minute later they came out, Ms. Pennington walking between them."

"Did either have his hands on her person?" Bret asked in a deceptively mild voice.

"No, sir. I asked what was going on and they told me to—umm back off. I told them I was her bodyguard and if she was leaving I'd escort her. Showed them my identity, they still wanted to argue so I took out my phone to call the police. They weren't happy about it, but shut up and we all rode down to the ground floor together. I didn't like the smell of it, so when she told me they'd canned her for no reason, I suggested we pick up whatever she needed from her apartment and come to your place."

Gaby smiled. "Suggested pretty strongly. And wouldn't let me drive my truck even after they examined it thoroughly."

"Thank you, Trip. You did the right thing." Bret nodded for him to go back outside.

Jon looked around at the other puzzled faces. "But what does it mean? Surely the partners were just being over-the-top cautious, never mind how it would affect Gaby?"

"Maybe. But did any of you see the news clip this morning about our County Commission Chairman?"

When all but Dana and Willa shook their heads, he told them about the arrest of the chairman and his reported request for protection in a secure prison facility. And Yates Orton's possible suicide in his cell.

"Someone may be eliminating witnesses. I want everyone to stay here in this house for the next few days. We may be a little crowded, but it's better to be safe."

He stood up and caught his wife's eye. "Think we could break out the food now? When it's ready the guards can take turns getting their lunch. I'm going to call Sergeant McAlester and see what he thinks."

"Of course. Willa, will you and the girls begin? I'd like to speak with Bret for a moment."

No one in the room figured Bret looked forward to that conversation.

***

When their bedroom door closed behind them, Dana went to sit on the side of the bed. Bret followed, sat beside her and took her hand. "I am sorry, honey. It was a knee-jerk reaction, wanting to protect you from something that would upset you."

"Yes. It was. And I don't want to be an ungrateful—umm—woman."

"Forgive me this time?"

"Promise me. No. More. Secrets."

He held her close. "Promise."

Chapter Forty

An hour later the food had been eaten, leftovers put away and dishes cleared when the doorbell rang.

Bret opened the door and Sheriff Glass, Sergeant McAlester and GBI Special Agent Sid Widner entered the foyer. When they filed into the living room Bret was not surprised that McAlester's gaze lingered for a second on Gaby as he checked all occupants of the room. Unless Bret had misread his daughter, the handsome, dark-haired Atlanta detective had a bit of competition in Trip, the cool, blonde security guard.

Never mind any budding romances. His attention returned to his old friend, Sheriff Glass. Jon and Billy had brought chairs from the dining room to the living room and Bret waved the lawmen to them. "What brings you all out, Cal?"

"I'm sure all of you know by now that Chairman Manchester has been arrested, and you can guess the charges, though that info hasn't been released to the press.

"Sergeant McAlester has been sort of liaison between us county cops and the Georgia Bureau of investigation. Agent Widner here has taken the lead on their end of things. So I'll let him tell you as much as he can at the moment."

Agent Widner looked at Heather. "First, I heard about the accident on the set of your photo shoot, Ms. Kenyon. I trust your injury is not serious?"

"Thankfully, no. I'll be fine."

"Good. Your former employers, as you know, were arrested a month or so ago on a list of criminal charges. As it turned out the most serious ones seemed to lead only to Mrs. Netria Fontenburg. Her husband, Dave Fontenburg, was not anxious to spend time behind bars, but he also seemed afraid to turn state's evidence. He was pretty shaken up when he learned of Mr. Orton's death. He doesn't believe it was suicide. It seems after his attorney told him about the arrest of

Mr. Manchester, Mr. Fontenburg wanted to come clean if he was given protection."

"Did he tell you anything useful?"

The agent nodded. "Mr. Fontenburg had decided to follow the example of his one-time girlfriend, Susan Kenyon, my apologies if this is painful to you her children, and began keeping detailed records. Subpoenas have been issued and arrests are underway." He turned toward Gaby. "May I ask why you are here in Georgia, Ms. Pennington? I understood you had accepted an internship position with the Eiler and Bentz law firm in Nashville."

"So I did. I was summarily dismissed when I went in to work this morning."

"And what reason did they give for firing you?"

Gaby's lips twisted in a sour grin. "That my being in their office might bring danger to their employees since I required bodyguards."

"I see. You might be interested to know that an hour after they booted you, both senior partners and their administrative assistants were placed under arrest by the Tennessee Bureau of Investigation."

Gaby's hand flew to her mouth.

Both Jon and Willa exclaimed, "What?"

Bret, Dana and Heather stared at the agent, waiting for him to say more.

"I'm sorry. I cannot elaborate, since the case spans a number of jurisdictions. I've no doubt it will land under the authority of a Federal agency or agencies since it has involved transportation of females across state lines for sexual activity."

The trio of law enforcement officers took their departure ten minutes after the shocking announcement of the arrests in Nashville. Bret walked outside with them and asked them one more question. "What about the man who kidnapped my pilot and his sister, held him at Orton's place and beat him and left him for dead?"

Sheriff Glass gave an irritated grunt. "Unfortunately he will not be standing trial.

"Why not? If he's been identified." Bret demanded.

"He's already paid the ultimate penalty. Unknown to Orton, who destroyed the one he found, and thanks to our lab tech, a backup copy of the test results of the blood under your daughter's fingernails led to his identity. He was a John Doe in a small town morgue in northwest Florida."

Dana joined her husband and Glass on the steps and watched as the dark blue state car carrying Agent Widner and Sergeant McAlester moved down the drive.

She leaned against Bret's shoulder. "Who could have imagined the branching secret tentacles from Sweetwater County to such a despicable organization?"

"Can happen anywhere, Dana, unless decent people run for office and win. I'd be pleased if one of you two, or both, did that." Sheriff Glass grinned. "And when Gaby gets her law license, she could stand for district attorney. Start a whole new family dynasty."

Dana's eyes widened, then a thoughtful expression crossed her face. "Grandpa Tucker used to take me to election rallies when I was a young girl."

ABOUT THE AUTHOR

Sylvia Nickels lives and writes in the Appalachian foothills of East Tennessee. Several of her novels and some of her short stories are set in that beautiful area. She is a member and webmaster for Lost State Writers Guild.

Sylvia has published two mystery novel series.
Requiem for a Party Girl, *Delusion for a Lonely Girl* and *Anguish for a Wounded Girl* feature female private investigator Cameron Locke.
The first book in her other series, Disguise for Death, features Royce Thorne, and was released by The Wild Rose Press.

For a few years Sylvia wrote a weekly column for a local newspaper called *Life Slices*. A collection of those columns, *Life Slices, A Medley of Musings after Three Score and More*, is available on Amazon and other online venues. Her memoir, *Eight Miles of Muddy Road*, recounts her childhood as a sharecropper's daughter in rural Georgia, and is also available from online venues.

Other books include *Best Served Cold, Revenge a la Carte*, a collection of her short mystery fiction, *Love Comes Home* (under pen name, Mallory Marrs), *Ringer Blues* novelette and *Just Deserts* flash fiction, all available as ebooks.

Connect with Sylvia through several places online:

Writing Blog:
http://www.mysterylanerambler.blogspot.com/
Writing website: http:www.ramblinscribe.com

Sylvia's Personal Blog:
http://www.postoakchronicles.blogspot.com
/Personal Website:
http://www.sylvianickels.com/